About the Author

Kim Hopkinson was born in North London and from a young age, enjoyed writing poetry and stories. She trained in journalism and worked on women's magazines in London. When she had a family, she discovered a love for teaching and became an infant school teacher. Later, she was a deputy head and headteacher and spent twenty years in education. Kim retired early to concentrate on her writing and moved to Sussex where she lives with her family. This is her first book, and she spends her time writing, raising sheep and enjoying her granddaughters.

THE REFUGEE

Kim Hopkinson

THE REFUGEE

Vanguard Press

VANGUARD PAPERBACK

© Copyright 2025
Kim Hopkinson

A CIP catalogue record for this title is available from the British
Library.

ISBN 978-1-83794-708-9

Vanguard Press is an imprint of
Pegasus Elliot Mackenzie Publishers Ltd.
www.pegasuspublishers.com

First Published in 2025

Vanguard Press
Sheraton House Castle Park
Cambridge England

Printed & Bound in Great Britain

Dedication

This book is dedicated to Gary for always encouraging me to follow my dreams. Also to Charlie, Lauren, Dan, Scarlett and Isabelle, my wonderful family, for supporting and believing in me.

Chapter 1
Murder in the Cornfield

Desensitised to the horror and gore of murder, that is how I felt. For there was a lot of blood, and so it is not for the squeamish. War will do that to you. Make the most horrific scene seem mundane, every day. But this was not war.

At my feet lay the bodies of a beautiful young, blonde woman and her son. Side by side, they lay like a tableau in a renaissance painting, ethereal in their death pose. If it had not been for the blood, you might have thought they were simply sleeping. I glanced around to make sure no one had seen me, but when I looked back, it was like a jigsaw puzzle that had been cut into many macabre pieces and jumbled, so they made no sense. The axe had made so many cuts.

So how did it come to this, you might ask? But you will receive no answer, for I have none. One moment I was crossing the cornfield with its ripening corn growing and swaying in the September breeze, and then I saw the mother and child walking towards me. There was a crack of thunder in the distance and a slight fall of rain, and I looked up. When I looked down again, they were lying at my feet, and the deed had been done.

That seems simplistic, like the slaughter of unsuspecting livestock. Back on the farm a million years ago, I never had any qualms about killing the animals we needed to eat – a chicken for the pot or a rabbit to be skinned. Was the motive for the murders sexual or for some kind of material gain? No. There was no motive; it just happened. I have no excuse.

What about DNA? You might think. Yes, that was exactly what I thought as I examined the carnage I had created. The cornfield stained with the blood of the innocent. The English police force has science at their fingertips. They will find me, as I am bound to have left fibres from my clothing on the bodies, or perhaps my blood. Although my victims did not really have a chance to fight back and I was not injured, but what about hair or fingerprints? Well, perhaps the identifying of these things takes time. I am in no hurry. Do I deserve to be caught? Yes I do, but I do not want to be captured. I know I have to get away. Far away, and I am used to moving from place to place.

You might wonder why I killed a helpless mother and child, and I do ask myself this, but all I can think is that it was the storm affecting the neutrons in my brain. Why else would I do it? I have no logical reason for it and I gained nothing from it. I did take a little keepsake to remind me of what I had done. Just in case later I thought that I had imagined the whole episode – a string bracelet or a friendship band that the child was wearing. I have made it larger and wear it every day to remind me. But it is not as a trophy, as I believe some killers keep; no, it is more a penance.

When I look at it I think of the tiny wrist it graced.

How I bent down and undid the small knot that kept it fastened. I turned over the soft hand that only minutes before had slipped gracefully from the larger hand of the mother. I stroked the soft skin of the palm and examined the lifeline that ran faintly across it. I was a thief who had stolen the future of this innocent child. The mother may have deserved to die, but the child. I had no excuse.

I said that I wore my keepsake as a penance, but that is the wrong word, for I feel no remorse. They were just in my way.

Not in a physical sense, for as I crossed the corn field, they moved aside from the public footpath to let me pass. I was in a hurry, moving purposefully. They were taking their time; the rain had just started to fall, and they laughed as they pulled up their hoods, and the mother crouched down to help the little boy button up his coat. Country people, ready for all weathers, or perhaps holiday makers, there had been more of these recently; it was difficult to tell which. I had passed them, and just then the thunder rumbled, and then minutes later the lightening crashed across the sky. That was my cue, or, was it the Mother's movement; bending down revealing the curve of her neck and the vulnerability of the top of her head – or the child's sunny smile, happy, whatever the weather. Why didn't I just keep walking? But no, I turned back and slid the axe from inside my coat, and after the initial blow, I found it hard to stop. As the rain began to pour, it spread the blood across the ground in a pool. I had a flashback to a scene in my village when lives had been taken and blood spilt, but quickly it was gone, and I wiped the axe off with a

11

handkerchief in my pocket and put it back inside my coat.

The walk back was a long way; I did not chance riding the bus in case the blood was visible on my clothes. Instead, my boots splattered the mud and flattened the stalks of the corn as I made my way along the side of the field. The rain was heavy now, and as I trudged on, I saw the steamed windows of the bus as it passed. I kept my head down and tried to shelter behind the hedges so that I would not be seen. I could imagine the damp, warm interior of the bus as its break lights glowed on the bend. When it had gone, I turned my face skywards and let the rain wash my face like a shower of absolution. If only the rain could wash away all our sins, but as I looked down at my hands, I saw the lifeblood of my two latest victims staining me, marking me as another, running into the crevices of my work worn hands.

Chapter 2
The Young Farmer

The refugees walk along the pavements in packs, four or five at a time, with their tanned faces and outlandish clothes, against the backdrop of an English village. Never riding the bus, walking the 2 miles to the local shop and 2 miles back, laden with shopping for the week. Not wasting their hard-earned money. As if carrying some shopping a few miles is no hardship compared to those they have already faced.

In the long grass, the children and the butterflies play, not knowing of the danger that lurks nearby. The farmer riding the tractor in the distance watches suspiciously as they trail along the pavement next to the field he is harvesting. As he runs his hand through his blonde cropped hair, he thinks the children's mothers should keep a closer eye on the youngsters just as he does on the calves and lambs on the farm. Don't they know that you need to be vigilant? Predators come in many forms, he thinks, and then dismisses the thought as being overly dark as he turns the huge monster of a machine and heads down the next row. On a wonderfully bright day like today, he has no time for such ruminating. He needs to get the whole field cut and the crop brought in before teatime while the weather holds.

The locals range from overtly suspicious to friendly. Many resent the infiltration of the refugees into the midst of village life, and others see them as a necessary evil if crops are to be harvested and local industry to thrive. Local people don't want to work on the land for a pittance when they can travel to the local town and earn double. Others feel for the refugee's plight living so far from home in accommodation that is basic and unwelcoming. Whatever the general feeling, the refugees are not moving on any time soon, so it is a question of living with them. What affect, will Brexit have on the influx of this cheap labour is a hot topic of conversation amongst the locals.

Bernard, the farmer, spends the day harvesting his crop and the evening transporting it back to the barn. He has had a good day and has worked late, but will the weather hold so he can gather in the rest of his crops tomorrow. He is not sure.

He has a terrible sense of foreboding as he makes his final journey of the day back to the farmhouse, where his wife will be waiting with a good home-cooked meal. He smiles as he thinks of the children playing with their toys after a day at school. This life can be hard work, he thinks, but it is worth it to go home to a family like mine.

Chapter 3
News

Once I had negotiated the lanes and fields without being seen, I returned to the worker's village where I had been staying since arriving in the area. In my cabin, I take off my coat, my trousers and top and put them in a black sack for burning later. I stow them under my bed, and having showered and scrubbed my stained skin and made sure no traces of my crime could be seen, I went over to the communal area.

Later that evening, the television in the lounge is reporting the National News; it seems there has been a murder right near where we are. And so I learn about the people I have killed. Sally Armstrong was thirty, and little Joshua was only four years old. Local people after all, living in a farmhouse with Sally's husband Bernard and her older son Harry. How lucky for him that he had not been with his mother on her walk. He had been at school, and that had saved him. It felt wrong somehow. like he should have been there too. A mother would not have wanted to be parted from her son, and what of the father would he want to exact his revenge? It was difficult to tell with British people they do not show their emotions the way we do.

Even so, I decided to put off burning my blood-soaked

clothes and boots for a few days. It wouldn't do to start acting suspiciously, even if I am keen to move on. There is something I must do first.

So, I simply carry on as normal, travelling to work on the mini-bus, getting my wages on a Friday, and buying cheap liquor at the weekend. Living in this seaside village is a strange existence. The locals do not want us here, and there is no interaction. We simply stick to others like us. Visiting the supermarket in packs and carrying our food home to the shacks, which were once holiday chalets which, now serve to house the race of intransient workers. We are bussed out to the farms and nurseries of the surrounding countryside to provide the much-needed labour – picking fruit and vegetables and tending the crops.

It is only when a job is mentioned on the other side of the county that I think perhaps putting some space between me and the murder might be a good idea. The police have started house-to-house enquiries, and it won't be long before they question the farmer where I work about the workers he employs. He won't be keen to share information. We work for below the minimum wage, and we are definitely 'off the books' as they say.

I ring the number displayed on the notice board in the reception and find that I can start at the new place in two weeks. That gives me time.

Chapter 4
Burning the Clothes

The flames climbed higher into the night sky, and the cinders blew away in the wind, sending sparks across the blackness. Paraffin was a good accelerator; everything burnt in a blaze of light, and when it was over ash was all there was to show for my evening's work. I stamped on the scorched remains with my new boots. I had tossed the old boots unto the fire with my blood-sodden clothes. Now there was nothing to link me to the murder except the axe, which I had cleaned carefully with bleach and replaced in my employer's workshop. There were so many tools there that no one would have noticed its absence for a few days.

In the distance, I could see the headlights of cars travelling to the nearby town. But the road was bordered by the hedgerow, and my deeds went unmarked and unseen. What would they have seen anyway – a man tending a fire, walking this way and that, poking the rising flames with a stick to ensure the garments burnt completely? The smoke rose into the starlit sky, sending a message to those who could read it. Look here. This is the man you want, the man who has murdered the innocent and who now hides his deed with the help of this fire.

The closeness of the flames brought a sweat to my brow. I wiped my head with the back of my hand and felt the thread of the friendship bracelet glide over my forehead. It felt like I had scorched my skin with the child's trinket. A reminder of what I had done and why I was here. Hastily, I pulled on my gloves, extinguished the glow of the fire as much as possible, and headed back to the country lane that ran alongside the field. By the time I reached the compound, I had built up a sweat with my vigorous walk back. Physical exertion gave me some relief from the images in my head. If only I could run along the beach and just keep going until exhaustion gave me relief from my own thoughts. But I didn't want to call suspicion down on my head.

Instead, I strode through the camp straight to my accommodation and once inside locked the door and threw myself down on the bed. I knew that sleep would escape me, but here at least I felt shielded from prying eyes.

I knew I was taking a chance burning my clothes, but people here often made fires in their back gardens, and I made sure I was well away from any houses or roads. The pyre of my belongings had made me feel cleansed and slightly excited. I was outwitting the police, and now any evidence they may have discovered, if they searched my lodgings, was gone forever.

Later, when I had calmed down a little, I made my way over to the worker's lounge and joined in with a game of cards with two of my friends. I shared a beer and watched some TV. If anyone asked what I was doing on this particular night, there were enough people to vouch for my whereabouts. I turned in at about eleven-thirty.

"Hey, Ahmed, was that you I saw out in the field last

night starting a fire?"

The words caught me unawares. How had Jerome seen me, and what else did he know? I was just walking over to the communal area to get some breakfast when I felt like I had been side swiped. Jerome's skinny frame fell into step with mine.

"Where you going in such a hurry? Slow down."

"I am going to get some breakfast," I answered, ignoring his original question.

"And the fire?"

"I don't know what you are talking about. What fire?

"In the field beyond the camp, I saw you burning something out there."

"Not me," I replied. "What would I have to burn? You must be mistaken."

He glanced at me with a quizzical look on his face, but I just ignored it.

"It must have been someone else."

I tried to look as innocent as possible, and he must have felt the anger coming off of me because he stopped speaking and the only sounds were our footsteps side by side as we made our way to the breakfast hall.

"I am starving." He finally piped up as we pushed open the heavy doors to the smell of bacon and eggs.

Chapter 5
The Locals

In the Royal Oak, the locals were nursing their beers, and there was a solemn feel to the atmosphere. There seemed to be a need to talk about the terrible murder that had shocked the whole community.

"Who would want to hurt a beautiful woman like Sally?" old Todd said aloud. "And that wee bairn he had only just started school. He was always laughing and giggling a lovely little thing."

"It's true," Joyce the barmaid agreed. "They were a lovely family. There are some evil people about. It has got to have been a stranger. I can't imagine anyone around here doing something so terrible. It is not like we are a hotbed of crime."

"No, the odd bicycle stolen, a domestic now and then, but nothing like this," George in the corner agreed.

"Well, the Police always look at the family first," the landlady Georgia added.

The assorted regulars turned to look at her. Joyce tutted, and the others frowned.

"You should be careful what you say," Frank the local butcher said.

"Bernard is well liked around here. He and his family have run The Acres End farm for generations, and I for one won't hear a word against him. Keep those thoughts to yourself if I were you."

"I was only saying." Georgia went on trying to retract her words. "No one says Bernard had anything to do with it, but when you read the papers, they do always look at the people she knew and who were close to her."

"Well, we all knew her. But none of us would want to hurt her and that lovely little boy," Joyce continued.

"No, mark my word, it was a stranger, and everyone should be on the lookout."

"When you say a stranger, have you considered it could be one of those strangers who are living amongst us – the Refugees?" Rory piped up from over by the slot machine.

"We don't want any of your racist bullshit in here, Rory. I have told you that before," said Georgia.

"I'm just saying. We don't know where these people have come from or what they are capable of. We have never had a murder in our village before, and they bear looking at."

There were murmurs from the gathered regulars, but no one replied, and Rory went back to playing the slot machines.

"I am sure the police will look at all angles," said Peter, a local landscape gardener who had popped in for a swift half on his way home.

"Well, they had better draft in some Police from the city as our local lads are not up to investigating a murder. I remember in the storm of 1975 a man was killed by a falling tree and killed outright, and that is about as close as the local police have ever got to a death," Frank continued.

"I remember that it was over Arundel Way," Rory replied.

"Well, I for one will make sure my doors and windows are locked and I won't be going out alone," Said Joyce.

Chapter 6
Refugee in the Church

It was draughty in the church; dim candles lit the altar, and the statue of our lady waited in the wings, surveying the congregation with a steely gaze. The village church was not ornate, it had only the one statue, and apart from the beautiful flowers, fresh and colourful, it was a cold and stony place.

The congregation were friendly, they shook my hand and welcomed me when the time for giving each other a sign of peace came. After the service, they went out of their way to make me feel like I belonged, inviting me to coffee and enquiring, where I lived and had worshipped before. When I snuck in at the back, I had not expected this attention, and I wasn't ready for their questions or their kindness. But an elderly lady had given me a hymn book and order of service, and she had helped me to follow what was going on. I confessed my sins and received absolution with the Lord's Prayer. If only it was that simple. I remembered the confessional box in my local Catholic Church that I had visited as a child, where penances were doled out – five Hail Marys and two our fathers, as if a prayer could take away my sins. The Father would look at my soul, and I would be damned for all time. There was no stepping back from what I have done. If only these people knew. It was not as though my stain is visible. To them I am just another visitor to their church. I was surprised the holy water hadn't boiled as I walked in. Looking up at the crucifix, above the altar, and the statue of Jesus hanging there, bloody and torn, I felt ashamed and cowardly.

Why had I come here? What was I looking for surely not forgiveness? I drank my coffee and talked with the priest, telling him that I was a long way from home and wanted to keep my faith alive wherever I was. The priest nodded sagely and told me I was always welcome in the parish and that they looked forward to seeing me the following Sunday. Would I be there? I did not know how long I would be free. The image of Jesus on the cross stayed in my head. Suffering to wipe away the sins of the world, perhaps there was hope if I could only stop myself from doing any more wrong.

All the way home, I kept thinking about how I had deceived those kind people. If I could only rewire my brain and think about good things and kind deeds instead of the wickedness that had infected my soul. The devil was real, and he could take hold of you and make you do evil deeds, but if that was so, there must be a God who counter balanced that evil, and maybe he could help me and stop what I was doing.

It was then that I thought about ending my life. That would put a stop to these terrible deeds and ensure the killing spree stopped, but I wasn't that brave. Why was taking another's life easier than taking my own? I knew it was a mortal sin to commit suicide, but wasn't it a mortal sin to kill another person? Of course it was. So my logic was faulty. Perhaps I am just a coward. I will pray to God to help me and show me the way, and visiting the church again could not do any harm, and it might help me to see a way out of this mess.

Chapter 7
May Greene

The cycle path was a find only really known by locals. The route ran off a local farm in a network of paths that circled the village. The paths were smooth and easy to negotiate, and the scenery breathtaking. The green fields were overhung by the vast open sky with fluffy clouds. In the distance was the cathedral spire and further on the South Downs in all their glory. It felt great to be out in the countryside with only birds for company – nothing to disturb the peace and beauty. May cycled happily for a few miles, taking the time to admire the scenery and remoteness of the path. Stopping only to open the gates or negotiate a stile. This route was new to her. How had she never discovered it before? She had not planned to cycle so far, but every time she reached a bend, she wanted to know what was beyond it. At one stage she did think that perhaps it would be a long journey back and maybe she should stop, but something kept calling her on. The winding paths might lead to a road, she thought, and she would be nearer than she thought to the pub she had started at. When she got home, she would look up the route on a local map. It felt like she was going back on herself, but she could not tell.

Judith, May's sister, raised the alarm. She was

expecting her sibling to ride over for tea at about 6. That was the arrangement they had every Tuesday. When she did not arrive, Judith called May's home but got no reply. Then she began ringing friends and even Judith's next-door neighbour. Judith cursed that May was of a generation who did not see the need for mobile phones and refused to carry one. Even when Judith told May that they were essential in case of emergency and that they were both not getting any younger, her sister shrugged her shoulders and smiled that lopsided grin she had, as if she was listening and agreeing, but would take no action at all. She could be exasperating at times.

May's neighbour Doris said she had seen her riding off on her bike at about four p.m. Judith guessed that May had decided to take a scenic route and have a bike ride before coming round for tea. She had done this on numerous occasions when the weather was fine. But now it was six-thirty and Judith wondered could she have been delayed or met up with a friend. That was the advantage of living in a village everyone knew each other, but it did sometimes mean that things took longer than you expected. Judith turned off the quiche that was browning in the oven and busied herself chopping vegetables for the salad. May would turn up sometime soon. Judith decided she should not worry, but the roads were so busy at this time of year. The population was swollen with holidaymakers, and the roads dangerous. She hoped May had worn her cycle helmet. It was true she usually avoided the main roads. Judith looked down at her hands and realised she was unconsciously wringing them. It had

27

always been the same. Judith was the sensible sister, and she had always looked out for her older sister, who tended to be dreamy and impulsive. It seemed silly to make a fuss, but by eight o'clock she was really worried and could get no reply from May's house phone. She began to ring people she knew who lived on May's route, but no one had any further information. It was then she decided that she would have to call the police.

They were very sympathetic, but said that perhaps May had forgotten the arrangement and that a person had to be missing for forty-eight hours to be considered at risk rather than two hours. When Judith explained that May was over seventy and that none of her friends had seen her, the officer had offered to come round and take a few particulars. He also said he would ask his colleagues to keep a lookout for an elderly lady. Judith gave a brief description of May and her bicycle. An officer arrived at around nine-thirty by which time Judith was distraught. She wanted to go round to May's house, a small stone cottage on Flint Lane, but she dare not leave in case the police arrived or May called. PC Dennis offered to drive Judith to the cottage to check that May hadn't had a fall or simply fell asleep. Judith retrieved the spare key she had for May's home and accompanied the officer in his car. May's house was in darkness, and having ascertained that she was not home and that nothing was missing, they headed back to Judith's house. The policeman called in the details Judith gave him, and a search took place. They identified May as a vulnerable person due to her age, and they enlisted the help of the police helicopter to sweep the area around the village. Even so, May's body was not found until two a.m. on Wednesday when the heat-seeking equipment picked up a person lying in the fields that ran alongside the cycle path on the outskirts of the village. A police car was sent to the spot and had to negotiate the single track that ran between farms in the area.

Judith never really understood how they had found her as her, body would not have been warm. She had her throat cut from ear to ear, and her blood would not have been warm for quite a few hours. Either way, she was found, and a tent erected over her body while the forensic experts could examine the murder scene and the body. Judith could not really believe it had happened. The shock was overwhelming. Her wonderful sister was gone. What a terrible end to her life. Who would want to kill such a gentle creature as May? Judith could picture her riding about the village on her bicycle calling out to people she had known all her life. A picture of her sister, riding a bike at twelve, on her way from their home farm to school, occurred in Judith's memory. Judith had contacted measles, and she had sat at her bedroom window watching her sister negotiate the muddy path. When she reached the far gate, she stopped and turned to wave goodbye to Judith before retreating into the distance. Where had that memory come from? She hadn't thought of home farm for years, and more importantly, what would she do without May? The tears ran freely and unchecked down her face.

Back in the field, May had stopped and dismounted to take a quick sip from the bottle of water she had stored in the small basket at the front of her bike. It was thirsty work cycling, and May had been going for about thirty minutes. The last part of the track was stony and unmade, and May had to go down to an easier gear to negotiate the dips and hills. She stood on the side of the track, taking in the views and drinking from her bottle, when she heard a rustling sound in the hedge behind her. At first she thought it was simply ground nesting birds and had turned to look where the sound was coming from when the man grabbed her and held her from behind before cutting her throat. He said not a word, and May's face showed surprise as she bled to death on the cycle path.

The newspaper headline read SERIAL KILLER AT LARGE IN SUSSEX.

Ahmed was sure there was going to be a picture underneath of him, but there was no picture, only photos of the victim during happier days, and the text said the police were following up on a number of leads.

Chapter 8
A slip of the tongue

As he sat at the breakfast table eating his cereal and reading the newspaper, he felt his heart racing and the panic sweep through him.

"So terrible, that poor woman and her child," Liam, who was sitting next to him, said, buttering his toast. "And it is not good news for us either."

"Mmm," Ahmed murmured.

"Where are the police going to look for suspects? They will look at the strangers who have recently moved here. And the locals are going to be even more suspicious of us. No, it is not good news for us."

He looked at Ahmed for agreement and nodded his head. He was finding it hard to speak with the pictures of his victims looking up at him with accusatory stares. He needed to get his pulse back under control. He didn't want his friend to suspect anything was amiss.

"I am sure they will find the murderer quickly. Perhaps he will strike again, and that will give them more clues."

Liam turned and looked at him confused. "Well, I certainly hope not. Two deaths in this sleepy town are quite enough. We are not in a war zone now."

"Yes," Ahmed said quickly and turned his attention to

his cereal before he said anything else that might give him away.

But Liam continued, "You know they are having the funeral in the village tomorrow; at that little church near the green."

Ahmed nodded and said nothing. But he made a mental note when Liam said, "It's at twelve o'clock. Shame we will be at work. I would have liked to pay my respects."

Ahmed was trying to think of a good excuse for not going into work the next day.

Chapter 9
The Funeral

The village came out in force for the funeral. Older people wore black, but there were some of Joshua's little friends in bright jumpers, as the Father had requested that they celebrate his short life. The coffin was tiny and white as it trailed behind the larger wooden one that contained his mother. At least they were together Bernard thought – always together forever. An image of Sally getting Josh ready for the first day of school came into Bernard's mind. How she had struggled being parted from her youngest son.

"But he's my little friend, and I will miss his constant chatter. I know he has got to go, but he doesn't seem ready."

Bernard had smiled fondly for his independent, fiercely curious son seemed completely ready to him. He wanted to find out about the world, which was obvious by the hundreds of questions he asked on a daily basis. It was Sally who would feel the wrench the most. His wife had struggled to make sure that Joshua set off confidently and did not know how upset his mother was. In fact, as they had both taken him to the school gates, he could remember how Joshua had ran in without a backwards look and how Sally had said, "Well that is that then," laughing before dissolving into tears. Joshua was still only part-time and that is why he had been out with his mother in the afternoon before they had to return to the school later in the day to pick Harry up. How Bernard wished his little boy had been full time and kept safely in the confines of the classroom and school yard for the day.

Now as he walked into the small village church, accompanied by relatives and friends, he could not believe it had come to this. The love he and Sally had, their youngest son, both gone. He felt a small hand slip into his, and he looked down at Harry, who at seven was fighting to understand this terrible thing that had happened, and his eyes filled with tears. He had to hold himself together for Harry's sake and so that he could see the man who did this brought to justice. That was the least he could do for the wife and child he had loved.

Inside the church, people were standing in the gangways, and many of the villagers had to stay outside during the service. Standing for the full forty-five minutes to show their respect. There had been a speaker system rigged up so that the congregation outside could hear the service. The media coverage of the murders had been immense, and there was huge public interest, but that was good. More people to keep a lookout for the murderer, but Bernard felt the public scrutiny at this time when he wanted to keep his and Harry's grief a private thing. As they took their place in the front pew, Bernard looked to his left and reached out to his mum and dad whose usually youthful demeanour had now changed to show their age and sorrow. He saw the loss he felt reflected in their eyes, and he leant over and hugged them. He sat Harry between himself and Angela, his mum, and they held a hand each. Then the service began.

As the priest started the sermon, Bernard remembered the day Sally and he had married in this same church and the joyous occasions when the children had been baptised. As he looked around, many of the same faces were present, and he felt the overwhelming grief wash over him.

Chapter 10
The Villager's Lament

Peter stood by the grave and felt a deep sense of shame. He couldn't get the idea out of his head that somehow this had something to do with him, and even if it didn't his behaviour had been reprehensible. It wasn't a word he used often, but it seemed to fit in these circumstances.

And what a hypocrite he was, attending the funeral, giving his condolences to the family, and generally acting as though this was not his fault. Of course you could say Sally was no better than she should have been, but that didn't help. What sort of man tried to blackmail a woman into having sex with him? A man like him obviously.

He had always thought he knew right from wrong, but she had become a bit of an obsession. They were on the PTA together, and as the parent of four young children, he was involved in various projects like the Christmas Fair and raising funds for the football club. And there she was all the time with her long boots and stunning body, making time to have coffee with him and laughing at his jokes. Until he had convinced himself that she felt the attraction too. As a landscape gardener, he could organise his own work schedule, and it became a regular occurrence that they would meet up for a chat. Usually there were other mums around or the children while they watched endless swimming lessons and picked up from a variety of clubs.

He found himself thinking of her as he made love to his wife, Melissa, and finding excuses to be where he knew she would be. One or two of the other women had started to notice

"Here comes your shadow," that bitch Sharon had commented on one occasion when he had arrived at a bring and buy at the church hall.

"Melissa's had to go into work today, and I thought it would get us out of the house."

"On a Saturday? Your wife works like a Trojan."

"Yes, they certainly keep her busy at the health centre."

He knew he had to be careful. The last thing he wanted was one of them mentioning something to Melissa.

Then it seemed the stars were in his favour when they all attended a summer barbeque at the Simpsons house. Every year they held a party in their garden, and as he had recently landscaped their plot, they wanted everyone to see it at its best. When he saw Sally go into the kitchen, he followed her and tried in a schoolboy way to try and kiss her. That was his first mistake because it was obvious that she did not welcome his advances. Her face registered complete shock, and he knew in that instant that the relationship he had been building up in his mind was totally in his head. She pushed him off and told him in no uncertain terms that he should never do that again. Then she flounced out to join her friends.

Peter was devastated and embarrassed. At first he was frightened she might tell someone, maybe even Melissa, and then he started to get really angry. He convinced himself she had been leading him on, flirting with him, acting provocative. What did she expect? This was all her fault.

After that evening, he made a concentrated effort to keep away from her. He was terrified that she might disclose the pass he had made to one of the other mothers. Gossip in the village was almost an art form, and he was worried that his name would be mud. It was no good he would have to tackle her about it and ask her not to talk to anyone about what had happened. That was the plan, but it didn't work out like that.

The week before her death, Pete decided to pop into the farm shop on the way back from a job in Midhurst and try to catch Sally on her own. When he pulled up, Angela's car was not in the car park which meant Sally's mother-in-law was not working, and so he was expecting to find Sally alone. But when he entered the shop, he could hear Sally talking to someone. But she was nowhere to be seen, she was obviously out back. "Don't do that Jack. Bernard could come in at any time. I want you to leave."

"I am just an ordinary customer. Coming in to sample your wares." He laughed, and she started to giggle.

Pete walked quietly towards the stockroom, but before he could open the door, he could hear them having sex. She was obviously enjoying it if the moans and groans were anything to go by.

Pete made a quick exit before he was discovered. Now he knew why she wasn't interested in him. She already had a man on the side. Jack. Pete didn't know anyone called

Jack, so he obviously wasn't local.

Then he made his second mistake, he decided he would confront her and tell her he was going to tell Bernard. What did he hope to gain? He wanted to hear her beg him not to tell her husband and to be grateful when he agreed not to. How grateful was she going to be?

The crunch came the week before Sally's murder. Pete bumped into Sally coming out of the local co-op and making sure no one else was around. He approached her as she was loading the boot of her car with groceries. He saw in her face as she glanced up at him her annoyance and impatience. They had not spoken since the incident in the kitchen, and it was obvious that she thought he was going to apologise. She was brazen he would give her that.

"Hi Pete, what can I do for you?" she asked, not bothering to hide her annoyance.

"Nothing much I popped into the farm shop on Tuesday, but it seemed you were busy. Busy in the stock room."

"Yes, well, I was on my own," Sally said a bit flustered.

"Not totally on your own." Pete smirked. It was good to watch her squirm. Now she knew how he had felt when she rejected him in the kitchen – the embarrassment and the fear that people would find out.

Sally did not bite and said nothing.

"Yes, I was sure you had someone out there with you. Someone called Jack?"

Sally's face fell when she realised what he was insinuating.

"Having a high old time you two were by the sounds of things."

"Piss off, Pete," Sally said, her face turning to anger as she slammed the boot of her car and made to walk round to the passenger seat.

"Perhaps I could get in on some of that action."

"Not in your wildest dreams," Sally spat at him.

"Well, if you don't want your husband to know what you and Jack were playing at in the backroom, I think you should reconsider. Let me know when you decide to take me up on my offer."

With that, Sally got into her car and drove away, and at the time, Pete felt like he had the upper hand. Pay back for the humiliation she had inflicted on him.

Now, looking down at the recently shovelled soft soil covering Sally's body, he felt regret, shame and slightly scared that someone might find out what he had done.

Chapter 11
Jack

Jack sat at the computer at his desk with the city skyline a distant view from his office window; there were some advantages to being married to the boss. A corner office and a highly efficient secretary. Of course he had preferred the pert, little blonde who he had employed before Florence, but Lydia was having none of it. His wife was a shrewd woman, and apart from making it difficult for Tina, she had found fault with everything she did. Jack was never too sure whether Tina had left of her own accord or if Lydia had made it worth her while to go. All he knew was that Lydia wasn't happy with the appointment and had insisted on hiring the next girl herself. Florence wasn't exactly a girl. As she strode across the plush carpet to deliver his morning coffee, he took the opportunity to look at her stocking-clad legs. Very nice, but Florence was pushing forty, and he had a feeling that she was always keeping an eye on him and reporting back to his wife. He knew he had to be super careful in her presence. He thanked Florence for the coffee and returned his eyes to his computer. No flirting with her, even though he thought she might be secretly holding a candle for him.

He was reading some files of visits he had made recently to clients and wondering when he could fit in another business trip to Sussex and the delectable Sally. What was it about that girl that kept calling him back? Was it her sense of fun? He had never met anyone who was so on his wave length as she was. In another lifetime, she would have been his ideal partner, as they shared so many traits, but there was an understanding between them, and that was one of the things he loved about her. They both knew the score and were happy to keep the relationship light.

There had been other women while he was out on his sales calls: receptionists who were overly friendly and made it clear they were up for a bit of excitement with a personable young man, female clients who, after too much to drink on a business lunch, were open to suggestions of spending a couple of hours together under the sheets. Jack was always aware of such opportunities. He didn't look for them, he told himself, but they did seem to regularly present themselves. And what Lydia didn't know couldn't hurt her.

It wasn't as if she had not known what he was like before he was married, and he never promised to give up his philandering ways. To be fair, though perhaps she had expected him to behave once they were married as she came to the table with a lot more than he did financially.

He clicked off the file he was reading and went on the Internet and started reading the news. There it was on the front page of a national newspaper: the death of Sally and her son. At first he thought the woman in the photograph just looked like her, but as he read the caption and then the body of the text with increasing panic, he realised that this was not just some lookalike but the girl he had held in his arms just last week.

"Shit," he said aloud as he read further. How had this happened, and what was he going to do? Would he be a suspect in a murder case? Did anyone know about their trysts in the afternoons? A friend or relative might have been her confidante? If the police went through her movements in the last few days, would someone at the hotel come forward, perhaps a member of the staff or that woman who seemed to recognise Sally in the bar? Now he felt really scared. He could not afford to be linked with Sally's death. Lydia would not stand for it; this could affect her business, and that was something she would not put up with. He could be ruined. He took a deep breath and crossed to the cupboard on the other side of the room where he kept the Scotch. This called for something stronger than coffee. He had to think what should he do next. As he finished his glass of Scotch, he decided he should do nothing. All he could do was hope and pray that no one came forward to say they had seen him on the day of the murder. For on further scrutiny of when Sally died, he realised that he may have been the last one to see her alive, that is, except the murderer.

No, the best thing to do was steer well clear. No trips anywhere near Sussex for a while. He scoured the internet to find out when her funeral was to be held and felt a lump form in his throat as he realised he would not be able to attend and say goodbye to the woman he did care for. There was no way he could do that and not call attention to himself, with people asking how he knew her and for how long.

He continued to read how she and her beautiful little boy had died, and the horror of the attack made him feel sick to his stomach. The tears came unexpectedly as he felt their wetness hit his cheeks. He remembered her smiling at him from under the cotton sheets in the hotel room the last time he saw her. Someone must have been seriously pissed off with her to kill her in such a horrific way. But who? And then something seriously scary sprung to mind. What if Lydia knew about their affair?

Chapter 12
A Change of Scene

I pay for my board and lodgings, and I am on the Southern Rail train the following day. I have a couple of days before I have to start work, and I spend the time looking for somewhere to stay. A bed and breakfast accommodation is available at a good price until I see how the land lies and whether I can find a room near where I am working. Perhaps I will stay a while and then move up to London or further, even to Birmingham. It is easier to get lost in a city, but I will have to look for a different type of work, perhaps in the kitchens of a hotel.

As I walked the winding street of Brighton, I felt like an omnipresence, as if I was invincible, and no one could touch me. I rubbed shoulders with the people of the town, and they did not know that I was the killer; splashed across the newspaper and on their television screens. I did not speak but smiled pleasantly as I thought about what I could do to them and what I had done to my victims. In my own hometown, I was less than nothing. The regime had classified me as a foreigner, a non-citizen I was not allowed to vote or own land, but here in Britain I was just like everyone else. They did not know or care about the violence us Kurds had suffered. How every day was a struggle to survive where we were beaten, tortured and killed for nothing more than being from a minority. As I looked around, here in the sunshine, I saw people of many different ethnicities and races mingling together without animosity. It seemed amazing, and I wondered why I had brought the chaos and violence to my new home. This was supposed to be my dream come true, but the past just kept on reappearing. Pushing me to recreate what I had left behind.

The train ride along the coast had been soothing – green fields, crops, interspersed with glass houses and homes. Before the war, my family had been farmers with livestock and arable land; now my country was covered in mud, the remnants of fire and gunshot, with the odd dead body or limb dotting the landscape. The journey was tranquil, and I found myself feeling sleepy and relaxed. The last few days I had been living on my nerves, waiting for a knock, or a boot, against my door, but it had never come. Even so, I was glad to be leaving the area where I had committed my latest crimes. The motion of the train seemed to calm me, and as I alighted onto the platform, I felt invigorated and ready to start again.

The lodgings were basic but clean, and my landlady in this town a little too friendly with her questions, but I tried to appear easy going, and I smiled a lot as if I did not understand. The language barrier can be quite convenient some times. Even though in the six months I have been in this country, I have managed to grasp the language very well. It is a question of 'needs must' as you British say. It was good to crawl into bed that evening and block out the voices in my head that said I was living on borrowed time.

To sleep.

As I had taken my train journey from Chichester to Brighton, I thought about what I had done. It was as though I could not help but appreciate the beauty of nature that I saw every day, but I had to disrupt that beauty because it was at odds with what I know of the world. If that sounds like an excuse, perhaps it is, but it is how I feel. Just as in the moment of the storm, I was sure that my brain had been affected by the lightening. What do I know? I am just a human being, or maybe a monster.

I had felt like a monster the previous evening as I watched the flames of the fire I had built in a back field beyond the worker's village. This was becoming a habit, but it was necessary to dispose of the evidence before I left the area. I had made sure it was dark, and I was far enough away from the roads and houses not to be seen when I tipped the contents of the black sack, which I had been keeping below my bed for days, onto the crackling fire. I burnt the clothes that had splashes of blood on them. The warmth of the fire drew me near, and once the garments had disintegrated, I stoked the fire again and threw on the jacket I had been wearing the day the old lady had died. Crouching down on my haunches, I looked into the orange glow and conjured up a memory of the look on her face. So shocked and surprised. A sweet-looking lady with soft, downy skin and a flowery blouse no threat to anyone. Wrong place, wrong time, that was all.

If Sally and Joshua were my masterpiece, then May Greene was a minor work. Her death had no substance to it. Its impact only being felt by her family and few close friends. I thought of my own mother and how I had been grieving for her for so long. Perhaps now I could lay her to rest. And my little sister Sacha.

Had I really taken these lives for no good reason? Or was this my idea of revenge for the rebel troops bombing my family? These people in this new place had no connection to my home and my tragedy. And I had wreaked havoc on their orderly lives for what purpose? The sadness I felt was short-lived though. What had Sacha and my mother ever done – nothing apart from being born the wrong type of Syrian?

Chapter 13
Brighton

In the evenings, Brighton was a buzzing place full of students and visitors who frequented the cafes and bars. It was easier to stay hidden here as everyone carried on with their own business, and there was not the distinction of standing out that you had in a small English seaside village. You could walk to the local shops from my lodgings, and there was more to do in the evenings with pubs and shops not closing early but staying open until eleven or twelve p.m. This made me feel more alive and less worried about being caught. As night fell, I liked to walk along the seafront and feel the crispness of the sea air, with the lights of the fish and chip shops and the amusement arcades twinkling in the darkness. There were groups of teenagers hanging around and many gay men hooking up in wine bars and holding hands as they made their way home. I think I was happy here at first because I never took a victim off the street of Brighton. The people I came across did not fit the profile of the people I liked to kill. There were no mothers and daughters or lone women. I began to think that perhaps I had dreamed my past and that I had put that all behind me. In keeping with this new life, I took a job in a hotel kitchen instead of the farm work I had planned to start. It was one of those fading grand hotels that stood on the seafront. It had seen better days but still had an influx of middle-class couples who liked the grandeur of the high ceilings and white tablecloths in the dining hall. I, of course, was banished to the back kitchen, where I washed up, prepared vegetables, and generally helped out. I made myself useful and was quickly promoted from washing up to kitchen hand. The Head Chef was a man with a bad temper and a drink habit, but he was happy for me to help him with his duties, and I learnt a lot from him on how to prepare fish and garnish a meal to the intricacies of making a Soufflé or Brulee. I was a fast learner, and I quickly felt at home in the kitchen. The chef talked about sending me to College to improve my skills, but I knew this would never happen as I was too valuable to him just where I was. I should mention that I was sleeping with him at the time. It was not that I particularly liked men rather than women; it was just the easiest way to gain his favour, and it made life at work easier. Also, it meant I could move out of the squalid rooms I was living in and move into a modern apartment that he owned in the city. He treated me well, buying me new clothes and jewellery, but sex between us was a rough and violent thing. It was nothing like the relationship I had enjoyed back home with Kayla. I embraced what was on offer; the price I paid for a bed and a roof over my head. I had done worst. But you know that, dear reader.

I think I have misled you a little by saying I never took a victim off the street in Brighton, that did not mean that my appetite for murder had diminished and that I was cured of my addiction. For that is what I grew to see it as.

I could go for weeks and sometimes months not hurting anyone. Work took up a lot of my time, and keeping Gerard happy was hard work. He wanted to show me off and introduce me to his friends. This meant many social occasions where I was probably seen as sullen and non-communicative. Gerard did not mind, he seemed to think this was down to the language and my escape from a war zone. He would boast about how he was helping me to 'lay my demons' and he liked having a young lover on his arm for the other old men to gawp at. At work we never touched or showed any affection; if anything, we were totally 'professional', as Gerard would say. But on social occasions, he liked to be loving and indulgent. No one would know how violent the sex could be once we got back to his opulently decorated apartment. I think he thought I was a good influence on him, and he would call me his lucky charm. He was making quite a name for himself on the restaurant circuit; now that he had curbed his drinking a little, and with his new-found success came more money to spend on decorating and enjoying ourselves. I think he really cared for me in his crazy way, but for me, he was a means to an end. I could stay hidden in plain sight in this new community I had joined, and no one was thinking to look for me here.

But as I said, my crimes were an addiction, and even when I began to feel that perhaps I was safe, I knew that I would return to kill someone else. It was not that I was looking or planning to grab my next victim, it was that the time and situation had to be right, and as the urge began to develop, I would start to trawl the area looking to recreate the scenario I could see in my mind's eye: the woman and the child dead or bleeding, helpless on the ground and the blood seeping out, the life and light diminishing.

Sometimes I dreamt of that moment in the cornfield, me with the axe standing over the woman, and waking in a hot sweat, I would look over at Gerard and wonder what it would be like to take his life. It would be so easy to just put my hands around his neck while he slept. But then he would wake up, and I would go into the kitchen and fix his eggs and coffee, and I would let him nuzzle my neck while I prepared breakfast, and sometimes he would drag me back to bed for what he called a 'morning romp'. Later we would wander the lanes of Brighton buying trinkets; Gerard was a great collector of antiques, and then we would drink coffee at his favourite cafe before having to go to work to prepare for the evening rush. There was a sort of routine to our days.

That was until one Friday evening, when I was making my way home and looking forward to a peaceful weekend. I had just finished my shift, but Gerard had some preparation to do for the Saturday lunch the next day. We both had the weekend free, which was very unusual because we worked most weekends. When Gerard finally arrived home, he brought a friend with him. He was one of the men from Gerard's wider circle, and I had always had a feeling that he and Gerard were more than just friends. I fixed him a drink and told him to make himself comfortable.

Gerard came into the kitchen and put his arms around me and told me to leave the meal I had been preparing.

"We have a guest. Come on, I have fixed you a drink."

"I'll be in, in a moment. I just want to get this into the oven."

"I have other appetites you need to satisfy." He came up behind me and pushed himself against me.

I could feel that he was aroused, and I indicated the living room.

"What about Alex?"

"The more the merrier." He laughed.

It was then I realised that this had been his plan all along. I felt myself tense. What if the violence got out of hand? There was no way I wanted to join in with the games Gerard and Alex had planned. I knew that it was likely that someone was going to be seriously hurt, and I did not know that in an extreme situation my baser nature might emerge and I might end up killing someone. With Gerard, I felt able to control the situation, but with Alex, who was young, and stronger than me, I was not sure what might happen. With my previous history, I could not afford to get caught.

Gerard must have felt my body tense because he started to kiss my neck and slid his hand downwards. I turned round and kissed him on the mouth, pushing his hand away.

"I like it when it is just the two of us," I volunteered.

"It is just a bit of fun; he means nothing to me; loosen up a bit; you may even enjoy it."

I allowed him to lead me back into the living room.

Alex was lounging on the sofa, and Gerard gave me my drink, a large gin and tonic. I drunk it down quickly.

"That's what you need. Come and sit by me." Alex indicated the cushion next to him on the sofa. As I sat down, he ran his hand along the inside of my thigh.

"These are great jeans, where did you buy them?"

As I turned to answer him his hands slid higher and lips came down on mine before any sound could escape.

It was then that I knew I had to leave, and I felt my fists clench.

Chapter 14
Flashback

The light over Sarajevo was low and sweet, swamping the area with a golden glow. I was getting ready for bed, and Sacha was playing in the living room with a doll that she had from when she was a baby. There were not many toys in this makeshift house that was now our home. The bombing had wiped out most of the city, and the few possessions we owned and had managed to salvage from the wreckage of our family home were precious. Sacha was talking to her doll in a low, scolding tone as our mother dozed in the armchair. She was worn out from selling vegetables all day. The few pounds she had brought home would not cover much for the week ahead. Since the death of our father we had struggled to survive in a city where necessities were expensive and nothing was able to get in and out. We were just managing to survive, but as I stood in the bathroom, I felt suddenly grateful that Sacha and my mother were in the room next door, and I knew they were safe and still here with me. We had lost so many family members – from the shelling and the barrel bombs, from disease that was rife due to the bad conditions and poor food and supplies. I had a sense that at any moment those I loved could be taken from me, but in that minute I just felt blessed. Was it a sign of things to come? Did I know that this was the last night I would have the only two people I loved in the world there with me? I don't know.

The following morning I woke late having had a fitful night, and I knew that my mother would have taken Sacha to the temporary school room that had been erected in one of the buildings in the old quarter. It was said that a generation of children were not being educated due to the war. But my mother and I were trying our best to make sure that Sacha kept on going to school and learning. One day I hoped this war would be over and the children would need skills for the future. School started early and was only for a couple of hours as the sun during the middle of the day was too hot for studying. I decided to walk down to meet them so that we could walk back together. I put on my shoes and my hat; this morning was hot and dusty, and I started to make my way down the battle-scared road. It was then I heard the wailing and shrieking of the women, and my heart skipped a beat. School had just been let out, and there were the bodies of children and women lying in the road. Hearing the shots, local people had come running to find loved ones dead or dying. With a sense of panic, I ran towards the school building, looking at the bodies of children as I ran. It was on the rough ground at the foot of the school steps that I found them. My mother had been shot through the head, but Sacha's tiny body was riddled with bullets. I sunk down onto the dust and cradled her in my arms and cried until one of my neighbours came and helped me carry her back to our apartment. Then he arranged for my mother's body to be brought back too; some other men from our building helped him, for I was of no use. Hysterical and distraught, I could not think straight; all I knew was that I wanted to get even. But I did not know how.

Chapter 15
Glasgow

Glasgow was a strange town. In the evenings, the people were hard drinking and harsh in their manner of talking. Fights broke out regularly, and you had to be careful not to look at a man, or a woman, for that matter, in the wrong way. Violence was ready to erupt at any time. I always felt uneasy in this city. The tenements where I stayed were dark and dingy and seemed to look back to a previous era. The people had a way of looking at you as if they recognised something in you that was evil and vile. No smiles or welcome here. Life was hard, and skunk was easily available on the streets. At this end of the country, I felt I might be safe from the police investigation. If things got too difficult, perhaps I would take off into the Highlands; no one would ever find me there. But I needed to be prepared; the climate was harsh, especially for someone who was used to the burning sun, and not the cold wind and rain that seemed to descend on the city most days.

If I am honest, I often felt afraid in my new home – the glare of a red-haired brute who stood 6ft 2" tall in his stocking feet or the sneer of the women on the balcony as I tried to make my way past. I did not think of hurting anyone here. The women were too thin, bony and scary, there was no softness about them, and so I stayed victimless for nearly three months. I felt anonymous in a city where I was treated like an outsider, which was what I was, and I knew I was viewed with suspicion.

Maybe I deserved to be here, but it felt like a living hell. I knew not a soul, and I found it difficult to find work. They had a fear of foreigners in this city preferring to employ someone of their own race. Better the devil, you know perhaps. Luckily, I had some savings to live on and the money I had stolen from my time with Gerard in Brighton. It had not ended well.

The night he had brought Alex home with him had unleashed anger in my soul. Pushing Alex off me, I beat him and Gerard. Leaving a blood bath behind me. I took the money I knew Gerard had stashed in a walnut watch box that he kept at the back of his wardrobe, threw some clothes into a bag, and left.

I wasn't sure if I had killed Alex. Gerard was still breathing when I made my way down to the train station. In the station toilets, I washed my bloodied fists and gathered myself. The trip to Glasgow took hours and lots of changes. I thought back to the previous journey down to Brighton. I always seemed to be running away from something. If only I could find somewhere that I could be safe. Perhaps in a new city I would find the home that I was seeking. It was a question of keeping myself under control.

The phone rang as I got off the train, and retrieving it from my bag, I saw it was Gerard. At first he said he had decided not to call the police; he did not mention Alex.

Then he begged me to come back; he said he didn't care about the money I had stolen and that he could make everything okay if only I would come home.

When I told him that wasn't going to happen, he said the police had been to the flat wanting to talk to me about another matter.

"If you just come back, I am sure we can sort all this out and just go back to the way we were."

"No Gerard. You weren't satisfied with the way things were, that is why you brought Alex home."

Gerard began to cry.

When the phone call ended, and I think he accepted that I wasn't returning. I decided that I had been right to move on; the police were getting too close, and I could not afford to stay any longer. It was easier to make my escape, and Glasgow had seemed the ideal location. It was far away from the murder scenes, and no one would think to look for me here. Did I now have Alex's death to add to my list? I wasn't sure. If he was dead surely Gerard would have told me and wouldn't want me to come back. Unless he wanted to see me put in prison.

After a while, I realised I had made a mistake moving to Glasgow. I now knew that this was a place where I could never belong, and I wondered if it was even a place that I could survive long in. My hometown was known as the Kurdish Quarter, and though it was a war zone, I missed it and the people I knew there.

Finally, I found work as a driver for a mini-cab place just off of Sauchiehall Street. I worked nights and spent most of my days sleeping and eating. I picked up a wide array of drunks, prostitutes and other low lives that frequented the area. There were lots of drugs, and I was asked lots of times to deliver packages and pick up bags of money. I tried to stay on the fringes of the criminal underbelly so that I did not come to the attention of the police or the drug gangs who ran the area. This was not always easy.

There was no going back, but I quickly realised that moving to somewhere new was my only option. I needed to work, but the kind of work I was doing was not always legitimate, and I was afraid of getting caught. I had enough money for a train ticket to London Victoria and for a few days bed and breakfast, so I began looking for work in areas that were not too expensive. East London seemed to be an ideal choice. I could find work there as a porter in a local hospital or as an assistant in a meat market. But I needed to be there to attend the interviews. I decided to invest in a suit that I saw in the local charity shop. London would be smarter than I was used to, and I needed to make a good impression if I was going to get a job.

Chapter 16
New Beginnings

With a new sense of optimism, I boarded the train at Glasgow Central; the journey took seven hours, and I settled down in my seat to find the most beautiful woman sitting opposite me. Not beautiful in an obvious way, but there was something about her that reminded me of Kayla. She had long dark hair tied back into a sensible ponytail, and her clothes were neat and non-descript – no bright colours, just conservative and slightly old-fashioned for a young woman. She had a book in her hands and was trying to concentrate, which gave me the chance to examine her in detail: a good figure, her nails slightly bitten and leather shoes with a low heel. My scrutiny did not go unnoticed as she looked up shyly under very long, dark lashes and returned my smile. I tried looking out of the window, but my eyes kept being drawn back to the woman in the window seat opposite, and I could not help noticing that she was trying to look at me when I was not looking. This was a good sign, I decided; it meant that she was interested.

My next step was to make conversation, but this was difficult because there were two other people in the carriage with us, and I was embarrassed. I thought of waiting for them to get off, when I might have her all to myself, but then I decided that she might not be travelling to London and might get off soon or before our fellow passengers. It was now or never, so I leant forward and asked her if she wanted the window open. This I felt was not intrusive but showed I cared about her comfort. The man next to her lowered his paper and frowned at me, but she returned my stare and said that she was fine and did not really want the window open. I carried on regardless of the other passengers listening, feeling brave but slightly ridiculous. Then I asked if she was travelling to London, and she replied that she was. This filled me with excitement, and she must have seen my mood lighten as she went on to tell me she lived there and had been in Glasgow visiting relatives. Our conversation continued all the way to London, and I found out lots of information about my travelling companion. When we left each other at the journey's end, she gave me her number and said that, as someone new to the city, it might help to have a friend to call, and she smiled in a way that lit up her whole face. My trip to London had gotten off to a good start. I had made a new friend, and her name was Rachael Stone.

This city smelt different – the rain hitting the pavement, the street food and the stale air of the bus and taxi fumes. As soon as I came out of the Victorian exit to the station, the change in the atmosphere hit me. The noise of the traffic was loud and intrusive, and finding my way was difficult and confusing. People were too busy to stop and help me find my way. In my broken English, I tried to explain where I wanted to go, but they did not have the time or the inclination to help. They simply shook their heads and hurried on. Everyone was in a rush. Where were they all going? Were they simply dodging the rain and trying to find shelter, or, was this the pace of their lives.

Perhaps I was emitting a warning that I could not see; do not engage; this man is dangerous. But I did not see fear in their eyes – only impatience and an unwillingness to connect – like they walked around with a force field surrounding them. Do not enter my personal space, their eyes seemed to say. I had been right' the city was a good place to get lost. No one wanted to know who you were or why you were here. The streets were full of people of different nationality here following their own agenda, and no one cared or asked what that was. For many, this might have been disconcerting, but for me it was liberating. Here I could be anonymous. I could come and go without the nosy neighbours or prying eyes of the community. Gossip in the country was something to share and accumulate. Minding your own business was the norm here I was soon to realise.

Finding a job was not too difficult with my forged papers. The interview made me nervous. Wearing my charity shop suit and explaining that I had just moved to London from Glasgow, they accepted that my references, although patchy, were adequate. Little did they know that I had written them myself and sent them back to Glasgow for Shiad, the minicab owner, to sign. I was able to get the job as a porter, which I had seen advertised, and once I was in regular employment, I set about renting an apartment overlooking the canal close to the hospital. This was more like it. There were quite a few different races and ethnicities in the area, and I did not feel out of place. It was true the flat was tiny, but there were little cafes and bars to spend your money in and a range of food stores that sold international foods. The whole area was very cosmopolitan and had a younger vibe, and although my flat cost most of my wages, it was worth it to impress Rachael, the girl I had met on the train. At work, I had made a few friends that I could socialise with on the weekday evenings. At the weekend, Rachael would travel from her home in West London and make her way to my place. We had not been intimate yet, but I felt that we were getting to know each other. In my country, this would have been called the walking-out period, but I had no parents to supervise the process, and hers lived miles away in the Surrey countryside. Rachael worked for a publishing house, and her boss Oliver was always demanding she work late or do some extra reading at the weekend. But she seemed to enjoy what she did. It had to be more interesting than pushing people around on trolleys and wheelchairs all day. My work was less physically demanding than when I worked on the farm, and it was better paid with something called London Allowance. This was to make up for the exorbitant price of living in the city. In the evenings, we would walk along the canal, dodging the cyclists and joggers and looking at the canal boats. Often we stopped for a coffee or glass of wine, and then I would walk her back to the tube station so she could get a late train back to her place. We would kiss shyly before she left, and sometimes we would hold hands as we walked, but I never pushed our relationship any further. I had too much respect for her, and I did not want to spoil what we had.

Chapter 17
Bernard in London

Bernard stepped back from the curb as the traffic hurtled by. What was he doing in London? The crowds and the traffic were giving him an anxiety attack, even though he was not prone to these. He had only come up to the city as the police had wanted to widen the investigation and look at murders across the country. They had asked for his help and wanted him to look at a data bank of people who may, or may not, have been in touch with Sally in the days prior to her death. He was sure he could have done this in this local town as they were all on the computer, but he was keen to see if the case was still being actively investigated, and Detective Inspector Lawrence seemed to feel positive that new leads were still to be discovered. What if he had the key to why this had all happened? He had to help in any way he could. He owed that to the memory of Sally and little Joshua.

The lights had changed, and pedestrians had all crossed when he realised that he was still standing on the pavement and had to wait for the lights to change again. His life was like this since Sally and Joshua had gone. He found himself staring into space for what could be seconds or hours. Distracted. Time having no meaning for him, and his lack of purpose was evident for everyone to see. On the farm, his labourers had taken over the bulk of the work, as he found it difficult to make even the simplest of decisions, and the land still needed to be tended.

It was as much as he could do to get Harry up and fed in the morning and off to school. Initially he had just wanted to keep him home and close, but even he could see that his son would be better off surrounded by his friends, and with the help of his class teacher, they had managed to settle him back into a routine. It did not help with the nightmares, or bedwetting, but talking was never Bernard's strong point, that was Sally's department, and knowing how much a seven-year-old could take in was difficult.

Now he made his way to the police station not really knowing what he was hoping for. Of course he wanted the killer caught, but that wouldn't bring his wife and child back. Nothing was ever going to be the same again and by acknowledging that, he felt a deep sadness and the realisation that he no longer wanted to carry on each day doing what he had always done. There was no point. What was it all for? His family was gone.

As he followed the canal path, he thought about moving somewhere else, giving up the farm and spending more time with his son. Not to London, he decided it was far too busy, but perhaps abroad. He and Sally had spent their honeymoon in Spain; perhaps he and Harry could take an extended holiday, lay on a beach, and swim in the sea. Why not? What was keeping them here now? He thought of the many seasons he had tended the farm; he had loved the land from a small boy, but now it seemed like a hard master swallowing all his time and energy. It was a hard life for a woman, and he had been lucky to find someone like Sally who understood the demands he was under to make the farm work financially, but if he had his time again, he would have spent more time with her and the boys and less time worrying about the price of grain and the amount of rain that was going to fall.

Here, away from it all, he could see the farm for what it was. He always thought it had given him a sense of belonging, but now he knew it did this, but it also took some things away, like time and energy. As the evening breeze blew across the water, he looked over and saw a man holding hands with his sweetheart. They looked happy, and this struck at Bernard's heart in a physical way, like a pain or an ache, for something he once had. He could not help but keep looking, and something about the man was familiar. He was about 5ft 10 – not particularly large; his frame muscular, and his hair dark. He was obviously foreign, although the girl with him looked to be English. Bernard wracked his brain. Where had he seen him before? He must be mistaken; how would he recognise someone so far away from home? He had been to London only a handful of times. He dismissed the idea. He was just being fanciful.

The police station was sterile and smelt of the drunks and fast food that had been consumed in the waiting room. He gave the inspector's name and was shown into a sparsely furnished office. The inspector stood up and shook his hand as he entered.

"Mr Armstrong, thank you for coming in. I am sorry

to drag you away from Sussex, but I wanted you to know that we are working tirelessly on your wife and child's case and we have had some interesting leads."

He gestured for Bernard to take a seat. Behind him was a board with Joshua and Sally's pictures pinned on it. Bernard was thankful that they were not of the murder scene but of the mother and child in happier times. There were also some other photographs pinned to the board and the inspector turned around indicating these.

"Yes, as you can see, we are linking the deaths of Sally and Joshua to a range of murders across the country."

Bernard was quite shocked. It was true that the local police were looking at connections between the murder of his family with that of a local woman who had gone missing and later been found dead in his area, but he had no idea that there might be more victims out there. As he scrutinised the board, he recognised murder victims that he had seen across the country in the National newspapers. Could there be a link?

"Oh, I see" was all he could manage to say.

The inspector led him to a computer at a desk on the other side of the room.

"As I said on the phone, Mr Armstrong, we wondered if you could take a look at our database and let us know of anyone you recognise. There are people of interest here mixed with those that aren't, and we just want to see if anything jumps out at you."

Bernard nodded his head. "Anything I can do to help," he said, sitting on the seat in front of the computer.

"Can I get you some coffee? We could be here for a

while."

"Tea would be nice," the inspector explained how to move from one face to another and how to go back.

"Take your time; I will just go and get that tea."

Bernard began going through the faces. Some of them looked harmless enough, and others rough and frightening. He thought of the last moments of Sally's life, and he wondered if she was scared and if one of these men were the cause. Anger started to well up in him. He stopped himself and told himself that he needed to be calm and look very carefully if this journey was not to be a waste. He tried to slow his breathing and take control like his counsellor had told him, and it was then that he saw the man. It was the man that he had just seen down on the canal. He was certain. He quickly took a pen off the desk and wrote the name on the screen down on a scrap of paper and stuck it in the pocket of his jeans.

The inspector came back into the room with the tea.

"Any luck?" he asked.

Bernard hesitated. "There is a picture of a man that looks familiar, but I think I just saw him on my way here."

"Okay, show me which man."

Bernard hit the back arrow a few times until the man was revealed.

"It could just be a coincidence."

"Yes, but in my job you get to know that you need to pay attention to coincidences."

"Have you seen this man before today?"

"I don't know. I had a feeling that I had, but I am not sure."

"Think carefully, Mr Armstrong."

"And where did you see him today?"

"Down by the Canal as I walked to your offices from the tube station. He was with a young girl. They were heading up to the main road."

Bernard tried to wrack his brain as to where he might have seen him before. Nothing surfaced.

"I'm sorry, Inspector. I might have imagined it was the same man. I am not sure."

The inspector shook his head. Don't worry, Mr Armstrong, but if anything comes back to you about him, perhaps you can give me a call. He handed Bernard his card.

"Now, shall we continue with the database?"

Two hours later, Bernard was worn out and frustrated with himself. No one had struck a chord, and he began to think it was all a waste of time.

"Inspector, I wasn't there at the time of the murder. What makes you think it would be someone I would recognise?"

"Well, Mr Armstrong, sometimes we find that the murderer has been hanging around prior to the crime staking out the place, or afterwards they return to watch the victim's relatives and friends. It gives them some kind of thrill." He looked embarrassed even saying this.

The idea that someone was watching him and Harry shocked and scared Bernard. Of course he had read about this sort of thing, but now it felt sinister, and he just wanted to get back to his son to make sure he was all right. The inspector noticed the look on Bernard's face.

"Of course this is not the same in every case, and you should not worry too much. Just be cautious. The murderer may be long gone. As you can see, we have a number of cases across the country, so it may be that he moved on long ago."

Bernard nodded. "I am sorry that I could not have been of more help, Inspector."

"No, thank you for coming in. We will let you know of any developments."

The men shook hands, and the inspector showed him out. Back on the street, Bernard's legs felt weak. What should he do? Should he track down this man? He didn't know if he had anything to do with the murder, but he was a man of interest to the police and Bernard did have his name. Should he try and find out or perhaps hire a private detective? No, he should let the police do their job; that would be the most sensible thing to do. But since when was he known for being sensible? He wasn't feeling in a sensible mood; he was feeling like he wanted to tear the man who had hurt his wife and child limb from limb. Where had he seen the man before? If he could only remember.

Chapter 18
A Chance Encounter

Now was not the time to do anything silly. Now was the time to hold my nerve. At first I had thought the man across the canal was just another man enjoying the late sunshine and staring at a young couple in love. But as he came into closer focus, I realised it was Sally's husband. I had seen him on the news with the boy, appealing for witnesses to the murder, and of course he had been at the funeral. Perhaps that had been a mistake to go to the village, attend the service, and watch my victims being buried. I wanted to feel that it was real and not just something I had made up or dreamt. I had blended into the background and just been one of the crowds, but my olive skin and dark hair would have made me stand out amongst the villagers. I had not gone inside the church, but I had listened to the service from outside.

Then there were the days that I watched Harry being shepherded through the school gates – from a distance, of course. Why did I not just stay away? Why had I had to witness their grieving? At one time I had thought of taking Harry and reuniting him with his mother, and brother, but the opportunity had not arisen. His father and grandmother kept a close eye on him, and security at the school was surprisingly tight. Finally, I realised it was impossible and that I had to move on. This was all before the move to Brighton – a lifetime ago.

How had Bernard found me, and what had given me away? Saying goodbye to Rachael without making a future date, I hurried away. She looked slightly upset that I had said I would call her without making definite arrangements, but there were bigger things on my mind. I decided not to return straight home, just in case Bernard was following and did not yet know where I lived. So for the next couple of hours I wandered the streets, stopping at local pubs and bars and trying to work out if Bernard had been following me. When I was sure he had not, I took a very convoluted way home. Inside, I locked the three locks carefully and put a knife under my pillow before going to sleep.

Chapter 19
Rachael

I had been visiting Glasgow to see my cousin Moira and my aunt and uncle who lived in the city. I tried to get up to see them at least once a year, and Moira often visited me in London during the school holidays. Moira worked as a teacher in a school for autistic children, and she liked to come to London to visit the theatres and museums. As well as being relatives, we had been close friends since childhood, and it was with Moira that I learnt about boys and makeup. She is two years older than me, and having no siblings of my own, I like to think that she is the sister I never had. She does have a brother, Ian, who is a solicitor and who is married with two children. Moira has always said that she would never marry but would look after her parents into their dotage, but that doesn't stop her from wanting a life of her own, and so when she visits, we go shopping, visit expensive hotels, take tea at the Ritz, and generally have a good time. In Glasgow, things are a little more staid. On home turf Moira, is a respected school mistress, and her parents and brother would not like it if she were to gad about town, as she puts it. Instead, we visit a round of relatives, read a lot and take brisk walks.

That's why on my journey back from Glasgow it was quite exciting to find a good-looking man opposite me in the compartment and one who was so obviously keen to strike up a conversation. The boredom of the last week quickly disappeared as he asked me about my visit and where I lived and a host of questions that usually I would have been quite shy to answer. But he was obviously foreign and trying hard to find the words to speak to me, and it seemed rude not to answer him honestly. It wasn't long before we were deep in conversation, which is not usually the done thing as some of our other travelling companions seemed to intimate. But I found I did not care, it had been a long time since a man had taken such an interest in me. That sounds pathetic, as though I am simply starved of male attention. But the truth of the matter is that although I live in London, most of the people where I work are female, and the chances to meet young men are distinctly lacking. I do have a wide circle of friends, but most of them are married now or have partners. Of course I am invited to dinner parties, and the occasional blind date has been lined up, but I must be unlucky because either the man was totally unsuitable or he did not respond to me in the way my friends had hoped. I must be an acquired taste. Anyway, meeting Ahmed made me feel as though I shouldn't give up just yet.

That is why when he asked for my number when we reached our destination, I thought, *Why not?* What do I have to lose? A good-looking man who is obviously interested in me. But I know what my mother would have said, "He's a complete stranger. Rachael, what are you thinking of?"

My mother, by the way, is always warning me of the

dangers that can befall a single girl in London. And I am sure she is right. But I also think that if you never take a chance, things will never change. At present I feel like I am growing older and I am getting no closer to the goal I want to achieve – the same one that most straight women in London over thirty seem to be obsessed with to have a partner and children. Before I can achieve this, I first need to meet a man – not just any man but one who is compatible with me. Not easy. Men are either looking for friends with benefits or are just not into commitment. Meanwhile, my biological clock is ticking and there are all these other career women out there who have been concentrating on their jobs and having fun that they have left it a bit late to start the family they have always meant to have at some stage. They are my competition, and we are all wandering around in our high heels and uncomfortable dresses trying to look as though we don't give a fig when we obviously do. Sorry about that rant. But welcome to the world of the generation who want it all but don't know how to get it.

Anyway, Ahmed was a welcome distraction on my journey home, and it turned out that he was very interested in me. In fact, he called me almost immediately, and we went out on a date where he was the perfect gentleman. And we have been seeing each other ever since. We go to the cinema and to wine bars in East London, where he lives, which are frequented by beatniks and local colourful characters. He does not have a lot of money; he has just got a job as a porter in a NHS hospital, and I am not sure that mummy and daddy would approve. But I don't care, I am old enough to make up my own mind, and he seems like a decent chap. He is very kind and attentive, and he has told me a little about his life in Syria, and it sounds awful. I don't like to pry, but living in a war zone and escaping to Europe seems to have made him appreciate just being alive, and he certainly has made an impression on me.

He can be quite romantic and will bring me flowers that he has picked. I hope he does not take them from people's gardens. But anyway, he holds my hand to cross roads and opens doors for me. It is true; he is a little bit older than me, but I think he is very chivalrous. I don't know where this is going, but I am enjoying our outings, and when he kisses me, I feel like I want to stay in his arms forever.

Chapter 20
The Inspector

Bernard decided to get the first train home. He had thought he might stay for a night before the trip, but now he wanted to make sure Harry was safe and be somewhere he could think properly. That meant being at home surrounded by Sally and Joshua's things. His mind was whirling with the things the detective had said about killers stalking their victims and visiting their relatives. All he knew was that he had to keep his boy safe, and then he would work out what his next step would be. But the man he had seen on the canal kept coming into his mind. Who was he? And where had he seen him before? Did the police have any solid leads? The inspector had not indicated this, but why had he wanted him to look at the men on the computer. He must have had his reasons.

***

The inspector sat in the armchair by the fire. Melanie, his wife, had just brought him a cup of tea, and he was flicking through the evening news channels on the TV. Bernard's face kept coming into his mind; he looked devasted, and he was still such a young man. What did it mean him seeing Ahmed on the way to the office? Was this someone they ought to follow up on? When the inspector had pulled up his details after Bernard had gone, he found that Ahmed had been questioned over the death of May Greene, as he had been in the area at the time, so he must have been local to Bernard when the first murder took place. Was that too much of a coincidence? Perhaps something else would come back to Bernard.

In the meantime, it wouldn't hurt to pull Ahmed into the station for further questioning the inspector thought. No, it wouldn't hurt at all.

Chapter 21
Into the Darkness

There is a community of immigrants here, and I feel more at home than I have since leaving my country. I think I could make a life here. In fact, I am making a life, but is it too late? Are my old habits coming back to haunt me? Just when Rachael and I are getting so close and I have a steady job and a home. Perhaps that is the problem; maybe I need to move on again; by staying still, I am easier to catch, but the thought of starting over again is exhausting. Do I wish I could change things? I don't know. Every step has led me here. My addiction hasn't gone away, it just lies dormant. As I lay in bed, I could feel the blood coursing through my veins the way it did in the cornfield, the way it did when I lay in wait for that lady on her bicycle stalking my prey, my unknowing victims. Only in that moment of taking life do I feel so alive and feel some release from my sorrow. An eye for an eye and a tooth for a tooth is what your Bible says, and I intend to extract that.

As I begin to pace my room like a caged animal, the urges I have felt for as long as I can remember are still there. I dress quickly in dark clothes like a camouflaged animal in its own urban environment. Even though it is gone ten p.m., there are still the late-night joggers. Who is stupid enough to go out in the dark to keep fit? Those who work long hours or who cannot sleep like me. I notice her almost as soon as I hit the path, and I realise that I have been waiting for this moment since the day I moved into my apartment. I have worked out where the path narrows and how it is darkest under the bridge at the turn in the canal. The ideal spots to grab someone and the places where they won't be heard. It will have to be quick with no room for error. I will have to cover her mouth quickly so that the screams do not escape. I have to be aware that no one else is coming along the path if I am to escape afterwards. But I have become more experienced because of the number of victims I have taken, and this is not too difficult. It adds to the excitement. I jog alongside her and smile, and then take over to get ahead to the bridge, where I wait in the shadows. If she feels a bit apprehensive, as she reaches the blind spot of the bridge, it is not enough to make her turn round, and once she is in the dank darkness, I pull her against the wall and stab her multiple times before slipping her soundlessly into the canal. With any luck, she will not be found until the morning.

I make my way back to my room via the street above the canal. I climb the steps on the bridge and walk slowly and purposefully away from the lamp lights and glow of the shopfronts. Soon I am inside, and I take off my clothes and put on a late-night wash while watching TV. In my bones, I feel that it will not be long before I am caught, but this was always going to happen eventually. This half-life I was living was never going to last, but not before I take one more victim, I think, as I finally fall off to sleep.

The daybreak sees me wide awake eating porridge, a

habit I picked up in Glasgow, and ready for the early shift at work. I feel invigorated, no remorse for me. I suppose I get high on my own cleverness. I have outwitted the police on numerous occasions, and if the papers are anything to go by, they are no nearer catching me. That was a close call last night with that Bernard man, but today I shrug it off. I will be off by early afternoon with free time to do what I want. And what do I do best? I will find a new victim before time runs out. Before I leave the house, I look at the friendship bracelet that Joshua had been wearing and look at how worn it is. I tuck it back into my pocket so that it cannot be seen. Why did I keep it? Am I trying to flaunt what I have done? I ask myself, but I have no answer.

Chapter 22
The Sandpit

I work cheerfully and efficiently at the hospital, where people know me by name, and my shift is almost over when I see a policeman talking to my supervisor. He has asked for me by name, so I duck into the stairwell and make my way outside, cross the road and head for the park.

It is at the sandpit that I see them – a blonde woman and a tiny child. I am not sure if it is a boy or girl, as I am not yet close enough to see, but I know that I am meant to be here, and they are the next two victims. The mother sits the child on her knee and brushes the tiny feet with her hands to remove the sand before replacing his/her socks. The baby giggles, and the mother says, "Are you ticklish." They are laughing in total unison, and she lifts him high so that his little legs are kicking the air. I move closer under cover of the bushes, and that is when I see him. Bernard. He walks purposefully towards the sand pit and sits on a bench very close to the mother. She turns round, but Bernard is looking straight at me, and he does not acknowledge the woman. He is like an avenging angel, a protector of the innocent. In his eyes I see a steely anger, and I turn and flee.

How did he know what I intended? That I would be here?

Bernard had reached the train station and bought his ticket home when something told him he could not board the train. He put the ticket in his pocket and made his way back to where he had seen Ahmed that afternoon, and then he had sat on the canal for ages on a bench and waited. He had not had sight of Ahmed until this morning when he was making his way to work. The apartment was set back from the canal, but the quickest route to work was along the footpath. Bernard had spent the night trying to keep alert but dozing periodically. Seeing Ahmed, with his backpack, sprinting along the footpath brought him up short. It was early, perhaps five a.m., and he could not get too close, less he see him. So he hung back and pulled up the hood on his parka. When Ahmed arrived at the hospital, Bernard had followed to see which floor he worked on, and then he had gone down to the canteen and drank two cups of coffee and ate a bacon sandwich. After that, he crossed the road from the hospital and sat on a wall where he could watch the main entrance. Of course Ahmed could always leave by a side door, but he had gone in through the front, and so he decided it was likely he would exit the same way. And in this instance, he had been right. That was how he had followed him to the park, and then something had told him that the women, and her baby were in danger. Seeing Ahmed off gave him some sense of control and power – something that had been lacking in the days following Sally and Joshua's death. This was just a man, an evil man, but someone who could be stopped, and in that moment he knew that he was the man to stop him, whether it meant giving up his own life or not. But what was he going to do? Follow Ahmed around and stop him killing his victims, and what if next time he was not so quick and he got there too late? There was only one thing for it, he would have to stop him permanently, but Bernard's brain screamed back at him that taking the law in your own hands only led to disaster; he could not be judge and jury. Where was the evidence that this was the right man? Evidence would mean that he would be jailed perhaps for good. If he killed him, he would end up in prison, and then what would happen to Harry? No father and no mother or brother. He knew that his parents would take Harry, but it was not the solution. And then he realised he did not want revenge or the hate to take him over; he just wanted the man stopped. He took his phone out of his pocket and called Inspector Lawrence.

Chapter 23
Katie

Katie dragged herself out of bed and made her way to the phone to call the office. There was no way she could go in today. She made her excuses and quickly got off the line. What if they suspected something? No, they knew that she had lost her friend in a terrible tragedy, they would cut her some slack. Officially she had told them she had the flu, not able to explain the terrible depression and lack of motivation she felt, but what did it matter? She could never remember taking a sick day; usually she just soldiered on, but this was different: guilt, rage, and a black cloud that hung over her. When the police had questioned her about the last time she saw Sally, she had given them the bare bones. Sally and Josh had popped in on the way home for a quick chat and to arrange to meet up later in the week. Sally had seemed happy enough, and Josh went into the garden to play with the cat. Sticking to what actually happened as much as possible made it easier.

She did not mention seeing Sally at the hotel, the business meeting she had in the bar, or the argument that had taken place before Sally left her home. Why add fuel to the fire? But by leaving things out, there was no way Katie could tell the police about Sally's lover. Perhaps he had been the murderer. If only she knew who he was, but

Sally had kept that to herself. Well, in fact, Katie had not given her the chance to tell her about him or to explain, for that matter.

She could not believe Sally was actually gone. She felt conflicted by this; one minute she thought she was glad she was out of her way, and the next she felt immense sorrow for the lost life of little Josh and the sadness Bernard and Harry so visibly felt. If Katie was being honest, her relationship with Sally of late had not been good. Even before she knew about Sally's lover, she had felt that what had been a friendship had turned into something toxic. Sally had started to neglect her, probably because of the new man, and only seemed to want to speak to her to ask favours, like pick up the kids, collect a package for her, until she had felt like the relationship was all one way. It added insult to injury; there Sally was with the ideal husband and family and she took it all for granted. She wasn't really made to be a farmer's wife. Originally she came from London, and what at first had been a novelty began to be boring and staid. Even Katie could see she craved excitement. Why had Sally ever married Bernard? He was supposed to be Kate's husband, and the children should have been hers. That was the mistake she made sticking around to see them set up home and start a family; it was like torture watching the man you love make such a bad decision. And Sally was oblivious to it. At first she would invite Katie to BBQs and dinner parties and try to match Katie with unsuitable men. Of course they were unsuitable when all Katie wanted was sitting at the table opposite her in the shape of Bernard.

After a while, this had stopped.

Even Bernard had said, "For goodness sake, Sal, stop trying to fix Katie up she is not interested."

Did he know how she longed for him? Did he get off with having her obviously adoring him when his wife didn't? Perhaps it was an ego boost. Either way, Sally stopped her matchmaking and started referring to Katie as her spinster friend, which was hurtful. But that was Sally for you, blind to how anyone else felt except herself. She was a very self-centred person, Katie decided, and she deserved everything she got. If only she could remember what had happened on that afternoon. She remembered getting the bottle of wine out after Sally left. Their argument had left her feeling resentful and angry and frightened at the depth of her hate for Sally. Because that was what it was, inside for all these years she had been seething with the injustice of it all, and this was the final straw. Not only did Sally have Bernard, now she had another man on the side. She drank the wine and became angrier and angrier, and at one stage she decided that Sally would not get away with it. Then everything went black, and she could remember no more. What a copout she thought. Did I follow Sally and Joshua into that cornfield? But the truth was she did not know. She didn't think she had it in her to kill Sally or her young son, but the problem was she had no memory of the rest of the afternoon she had passed out cold.

When Katie thought about it calmly, she could not imagine herself using an axe to kill Sally and Joshua. Where would she have got the weapon anyway? It wasn't something she kept hanging around. The last time she had seen one was in Sally's barn. Bernard sometimes used it to chop up fallen trees, she thought, and then it occurred to her that perhaps Bernard had been the murderer. She wiped this idea away as quickly as it had arrived; after all, Bernard was so in love with Sally and he would never harm his own son. Also, Sally had known him all his life and had never known him to be violent in any way. She was more likely to be the murderer than him, she thought, dismissing the worry that was threatening to engulf her.

Chapter 24
Gossip in the local shop

"The problem is everyone is a suspect," Lorna said, holding court in the village shop.

"What with police men, swarming all over the village and men being asked to submit to DNA testing. What have they found I want to know? Do they have fingerprints or hairs on the body?"

She's been watching Silent Witness again. Mrs Donaldson, behind the counter, thought, but out loud she simply said, "I am sure the police are just doing their jobs, Lorna. If you haven't done anything, you have nothing to fear."

"Well, who says it is a man? Any way it could have been a woman," Lorna continued.

"Not with the power and force they used to swing that axe, the poor woman and her child did not stand a chance," Doug, who had just popped in for a loaf of bread, contributed.

"Well, I won't be letting them take DNA swabs from me," said John over by the newspaper stand.

"The police are desperate to find the killer, and you hear about innocent men being fitted up all the time and spending years in jail for something they never did. No fear, I won't be agreeing to none of that."

"That just makes you look like you have something to hide. Don't you want the police to eliminate you from their enquiries so they can find the real culprit?" Lorna was warming to her subject.

"No one wants the man who did it to get away with it, and it will be better when he is behind bars and we can go about our business without worrying, but John has a point, said Doug. The problem is once they have your DNA and fingerprints on their computers, you are in the system whether you want to be or not."

"I think we all have a duty to do whatever we can to help find the monster that did this to Sally and her poor little boy. And you men should be ashamed just thinking of yourselves. What if it was your wife or son?" Mrs Donaldson almost threw John's change back at him as she took the money for his paper. Looking shamefaced, he exited the small shop that was beginning to feel crowded, with a ding of the bell above the door.

As she closed up that evening, Mrs Donaldson thought about all the gossip that she had heard during the course of her day. Everyone had a view and their two pennies to add, as her mother would have said. Chinese Whispers were rampant in the village, and it wasn't very often that there was much to talk about. A murder would be discussed for years to come. She shouldn't be surprised, but Sally was one of their own. It was true she had been an outsider when she married Bernard, but over the years she had integrated into the village, took her place on the PTA and was a regular at church. You could always see her and her children about in the village and she would often pop into the village shop for something she had forgotten. It was true she did her big shop at the supermarket in town, but she believed in keeping local businesses alive and she ran the farm shop and so was a local entrepreneur herself. And Mrs Donaldson liked her, with her easy-going manner and sunny nature. One or two of the ladies at church thought she was flighty, but not so Mrs Donaldson she knew how fiercely she loved her children and how invested she was in the future of the village. It was a terrible end for such a beautiful woman and her child. No one deserved that, and Mrs Donaldson found her eyes welling up, and not for the first time since Sally's death. What was the world coming to, and who would do such a terrible thing? Well they all had their suspicions. And you didn't have to go too far out of the village to know where the murderer might have come from. Distrust of strangers was leading many of the villagers to jump to conclusions. In the olden days they might have taken the law into their own hands and gone looking for the murderer in the worker's village, but nowadays they had to leave the investigating to the police. Let's hope they find a suspect soon, Mrs Donaldson thought before he strikes again.

Chapter 25
Bernard asks for help

They met in a pub not far from the police station, and Bernard tried to explain what had happened earlier that day. He knew what he had to say sounded farfetched and perhaps slightly deranged, but he wanted to share it with someone else, and the inspector was a good listener.

"Okay, so you have no evidence that this man has killed anyone – just a hunch and a feeling that you have seen him somewhere before. Have you considered that you may have seen him in your area, as he was working there, or that you have just become fixated on this man? It happens, and I have to warn you that following someone could be construed as stalking, and you could be in trouble. Did he speak to the woman and child at the sandpit or approach them?

"Yes, I have considered that this might be all in my mind. That is why I needed to talk it over with someone else, and no, he didn't talk to the woman in the park, but he was approaching her until he saw me."

"Did he recognise you?"

"I don't know. I think there was some recognition there. Either way he stopped and went off in the other direction."

"So what do you want me to do?" the inspector asked.

"I really don't know; keep an eye on him perhaps."

Bernard knew what the reply was going to be before the inspector answered just by the expression on his face.

"Mr Armstrong, Bernard," he corrected himself, "we just don't have the resources available to follow people who might commit a crime."

"But this man could have already killed my wife and son, and how are you going to solve the crimes if you don't investigate him, and how will you feel if he goes on to kill other people?"

"I know what you are saying, and I do have every sympathy, but all I can do is to warn you not to do anything silly. My advice to you, Bernard, is to go home and look after that little boy of yours and let us do our job."

The words he was saying sounded hollow even to the inspector, but what could he do for this grieving young man. He was not going to tell him that they were trying to bring Ahmed in for questioning or that he was connected to the May Greene murder in his area. This would just add fuel to the fire. Bernard shook his head.

"Okay, thank you for seeing me, Inspector," Bernard said, rising, leaving half of his beer. Outside the pub, he dialled his mother to check on Harry, and as he walked back to the canal, where he had first seen Ahmed, she put his little boy on the phone, and he launched into a long explanation about a science project he was working on. It was good to hear his voice and his enthusiasm for his learning. Finally, they said goodbye.

"Daddy, when are you coming home?" Harry asked.

"The police just need me for a few more days, darling.

I promise I will see you soon."

Harry seemed happy with that. "Okay. Love you, Daddy."

"Love you too, Harry."

Then he was gone, and Bernard settled down for a long wait on the bench, on the canal, close to where Ahmed lived. He was lucky that the weather was still relatively mild. Even so, he was not relishing another night on a hard bench. He was just putting his mobile back into his coat pocket when he saw Ahmed heading the opposite way from the way he went to work. He was heading towards the high street, and when he reached the stairs up to the bridge, he mounted them quickly. Bernard on the opposite side of the canal found it difficult to keep up. Ahmed had a backpack on again, but this time it seemed heavier.

Chapter 26
The Ruse

The call to Rachael had taken only a few minutes. I explained I had found a rat in my flat, and it seemed that there had been a number of instances of this in the building, so they had called in the pest control people, and they were going to treat the problem the next day. I asked, as a favour, if I could stay with her for a few days. I was sure it would not take long. She had agreed immediately; the idea of staying in a flat with the rat made her shudder. Of course, I must come over and stay for as long as I liked.

If she was honest, Rachael was hoping that this would move their relationship onto the next stage. They had been seeing each other for a couple of months and had never progressed further than the kissing and holding hands stage, even though there had been plenty of opportunities. Perhaps being in close proximity to each other for a few days would change the dynamics of the relationship, for she had felt that Ahmed was keeping something from her. She hoped he did not have a wife back where he came from. He spoke very little about his past, saying that he preferred to forget it as it was full of sad memories. She had not pushed him on this, but she was beginning to feel that his past held the key to all the questions she had and would help her understand him better.

Rachael's flat was exactly as Ahmed expected: clean,

tidy, with flowery wallpaper and soft carpets. She made them tea and they spent the evening chatting and watching TV. He felt himself relaxing in her company and not having to be on his best behaviour as he usually was. She had made up the bed for him in the spare room, and he could not help but feel that she was slightly stupid for allowing him into her home. Like the sheep he saw on the farm, dazed and passive. Did she not sense the danger she was in? Obviously not; she had only known him a few months, and she was willing to give him a bed for the night. They talked about her parents in Surrey, and then she asked about his family. What was he supposed to say they had all been slaughtered; it was not exactly light conversation. So he skirted round her questions and said it was too painful for him to talk about. She looked slightly hurt by this and said that she really did want to get to know him, and that meant sharing things with each other. He kept quiet after this and was quite glad when bedtime arrived and he was shown into a very feminine spare room. Was he expecting something else? He didn't know. But it was a relief lying under the cool cotton sheets alone. Did she expect him to make the journey along the corridor to her room in the night? Surely that might scare her. He realised just how little he really knew about Rachael. Even with all the dates they had been on, she was still a virtual stranger.

Did he mean her any harm, and was this latest story of the rat just a ploy to get her alone so that he could hurt her. He thought carefully. No, he did not want to kill her. He liked her. She was the only one he had met since coming to England that he really liked. But did he want to take it further? He did not know. He was scared. There was no happy ending here. Not once she found out what he really was and what he had done. Letting someone in was not easy when you could not tell them the truth about yourself. On a date, lying was easy, but keeping the lies up and being always on your guard was hard work.

Just then the door opened, and Rachael slipped into the room and into his bed. Under the covers, he felt the outline of her body pressed against him, and words were no longer necessary. He was a man and he needed her and just for tonight that was enough.

The jogger's body was discovered by men fishing further down the canal at six a.m. that morning while Ahmed and Rachael were sleeping soundly wrapped in each other's arms. The identification process did not take long as colleagues at the offices where she worked had reported Catrina missing the day before, after she had failed to turn up at the bank in the city. She was supposed to be giving a big presentation, and they knew she would not have missed it. When they rang her mother in Madrid and she had not heard from her, they had contacted the police straight away. Living in the city alone, she was a popular girl with lots of friends, and when no one had heard from her since she posted she was off out on a jog on her WhatsApp the evening before her big presentation, they knew something must be wrong. In fact, she actually lived in the same block as Ahmed, a fact that did not go unnoticed by the inspector when he went through her details.

Chapter 27
Confrontation

Bernard took the stairs at the side of the bridge, two at a time and reached the pavement at the top slightly out of breath, only to be confronted by Ahmed.

"Are you following me?" Ahmed asked aggressively.

"No, I am in a hurry to catch a train," Bernard answered, refusing to be caught on the back foot.

"I've seen you before." Ahmed's lip curled as he moved closer to Bernard, and Bernard began to worry that perhaps he had a weapon – a knife or a blade. He stepped back.

"Really, where?"

"Never mind where. What do you want?"

"Nothing, I told you I am in a hurry because I am trying to catch a train."

Ahmed stepped out of his way and let him past, and Bernard, sweating slightly now, moved quickly along the high street. A glance back confirmed his fears that Ahmed was following him. Okay, so he would make his way to the train station, as he said he was, but where should he go? Maybe into central London, and hopefully he would lose Ahmed there. He would not go back home and perhaps lead himself and Harry into more danger, and he did not like the idea of going back to the hotel he was staying at; he wanted to avoid any further confrontation.

His route back to the hotel took him almost two and a half hours, and only when he was sure that he had lost Ahmed did he dare to make his way back across London. Once safely ensconced in his room, having drunk a cup of tea and a swig of Scotch from the bottle he had bought at the local off licence; he could feel his heartbeat slowing and his hand stop shaking. If he hadn't been sure before, he was convinced now that Ahmed was the murderer and the man the police should be looking for, but how was he going to make the police see it his way? They needed evidence and more than just his hunch. The man was obviously violent and aggressive if their confrontation was anything to go by, but thinking about it logically, there was nothing that linked the man to the murders, and by continuing with his current plan of following and watching him, perhaps Bernard would provoke a reaction.

Chapter 28
Back in the Village

Pete didn't know what to do. He looked down at the bulbs he was supposed to be planting, and he noticed that his hands were shaking. He had been in a state of agitation all day since he had heard on the grapevine that Bernard had travelled to London to help the police with their enquiries. What did that mean? Were they getting any closer to finding the killer? He hoped so. He felt like he was living on his nerves, and other people were beginning to notice. His wife, Melissa, had asked him if he felt okay this morning at breakfast as he was finding it hard to eat and carry on as normal.

Working outside in Mrs Matthew's garden, he thought he would be better able to think and clear his head. Instead, he found himself going back over his conversations with Sally and wondering how he had gotten the idea that she liked him. She was just friendly to everyone, and he had been an idiot to think there was anything more in it than that. And then to try and use what he knew about her relationship with this other man to blackmail her into a sexual relationship with him made him disgusted with himself. If someone had suggested that he might do something like that, he would have thought he didn't have it in him. But jealousy is a terrible emotion and something he had never suffered in the past. It had surprised him how much he wanted to hurt her.

And what about the other mothers at the school? Were they suspicious? He had not really been that discrete with his always managing to be where Sally was. He knew there had been gossip, and he wondered if Sally had discussed him with her friends. Would one of them suggest to the police that he might be someone they should look at? Could what he had been doing be called stalking? No, he had legitimate reasons for being at PTA meetings and other social gatherings where Sally was. He had children of his own and reasons for being there. Should the police ask, he could explain being in her company so much. And anything the other women said he could dismiss as simply gossip. Would the police buy that, or should he admit to an attraction to her. No. That was a bad idea; his wife might hear about it, and the police might see him in the role of the spurned lover.

Pete bent down and pushed the earth around the base of the dahlias he had just planted. If the police were to find out that he tried to blackmail Sally, they might wonder what else he would do. But they were not going to find out about his demands on Sally, as no one had heard what he had said, but what about the lover? He was slowly realising that by avoiding telling anyone about what had happened between him and Sally, this meant he could not tell the police about the lover he had discovered. Was he being a coward or simply safeguarding his wife and family? What could he tell the police anyway? He did not know the man's full name or anything about him, just that he existed. Would that help them to find the murderer?

He was conflicted; he knew that the right thing to do was to go to the police and tell them all he knew, but he was a coward and did not want to face what that might mean for him and his family. But a woman and her child were dead, and he might hold the key to new evidence – could he live with himself if he stood around and did nothing? Looking down at the shovel he held in his hand, he thought of Sally and Joshua buried in the cold earth of the graveyard and how such a lively and warm woman had come to a violent end. He stopped digging the hole for the next batch of plants. He gathered his tools and belongings and got back in his van and headed off. Working was not helping him get his head straight, and sitting at home was no better. He headed for the village pub to try and drown his sorrows.

Chapter 29
Interlude

Sally lay stretched out naked on the bed with a fur throw pulled up over her lower half. She had never known such luxury: champagne and orange juice at ten-thirty in the morning in a swish hotel on the outskirts of town. No expense had been spared, and the sex was amazing. Her lover stroked her tummy, which sent goose bumps down her spine. She turned over and pulled him to her. She was ready for him again. Was it because she had to pick Joshua up at twelve-thirty and she did not know when they would be together again, or was it the thrill of illicit meetings and sexy texts? Either way, she enjoyed the way he took control of her body and knew exactly what she needed when she needed it. Being a farmer's wife was not all she had hoped it would be, and with two young children and money tight, there wasn't much time for romance or sex come to that. Falling for Jack was such a cliché really – a travelling salesman of all things. A chance meeting in the local post office had led to expensive dinners and presents she had to hide from her husband. It wasn't as though she had any intention of leaving Bernard. She was just a little bored. She knew it was no excuse, but she just couldn't seem to help herself. She was as lovesick as a teenager, and Jack certainly had something about him. All she had to do was make sure that no one found out. She had not mentioned Jack to anyone, not even her best friend Katie. This was her secret, and she was being very careful. Jack always paid the bills, usually in cash, she noticed, and he was very discreet. It was quite difficult to keep finding excuses for spending time away from her family, but she always had been very creative. She knew that this could not go on much longer; it was leading nowhere, and she did not really want to ruin what she had with Bernard. She loved her family, and she had no intention of leaving them or him. This was just a bit of fun, nothing serious, so why did she live for the times when she could see Jack? He made her feel so alive and young. Not the boring, stay-at-home mum, that she felt at other times. The idea that she might have to give him up made her love-making with Jack all the more frantic and exhilarating.

Sitting outside on the forecourt was Bernard's four by four. He had parked over to the side of the lot so that he could not be seen from the hotel. It had been a matter of chance that he had seen Sally in Jack's car travelling out of the town towards Ashling. He was going into town to pick up a spare part for the tractor, and coming towards him, he had noticed a white Audi, going too fast, and in the passenger seat was Sally. Her head was turned towards the driver, and he was sure she had not seen him. It was the way she was looking at the driver that drove a stake through his heart. She was smiling and laughing the way she used to with him before they had the children. He did not hesitate, he carried on to the next roundabout and then turned the car around and followed them to the Swan Hotel just out of town. He did not rush; he followed at a distance so as not to raise the driver's suspicions, and he stopped the car before the car park, so that he could see the two of them holding hands and going inside. She was brazen, he thought, or stupid. Although the hotel was out of town, lots of local people worked there, and she would be the subject of a lot of hot gossip. His reputation must mean nothing to her. The good name he and his family had always had in the area would be gone. He would be known as the man whose wife was no better than a prostitute. He would never be able to hold his head up in town again. He was going to confront her and tell her he was divorcing her. She had always been a bit flirty, but now he realised that what he took as good humour was loose ways. How many others had she slept with? The sooner he could be rid of her, the better. But then he started thinking about his children. He did not want to be a weekend father living apart and relying on Sally's goodwill for when he could see them. He knew there was no way she would give them up, even if she thought that life on the farm would be better for them. The Farm, it suddenly occurred to him that she would want a share in the property that had been in his family for many generations. Why should he give her a penny? It was her fault they were in this situation. Did she even think of her family while she was shagging that man?

He felt the anger welling up in him. Should he go into the hotel, and make a scene and confront them both? What good would that do? he decided. What he needed was a permanent solution to this problem.

The drive home helped to calm his temper. He didn't

want to give up the life he had. He had to win his wife back; that was the only solution; perhaps he had been neglecting her lately. This might only be a casual fling he had to show her how much she meant to him.

Chapter 30
Caught

Sally licked her lips and applied some of the Channel lip gloss to her mouth, pouting into the mirror. The light in the hotel toilets was poor, and she pursued her lips together to make sure there was an even sheen. She adjusted her skirt and smoothed her jumper, which fitted snugly over her ample figure. Jack was waiting in the bar, and she felt a tingling sensation when she thought about their afternoon ahead. She hadn't felt so excited since the time she had made out with Bernard in the Hay Barn when they were first going out. The thought of her husband and how they had been back then made a shadow appear across her face. She had been mad for him, so what had changed? Life had changed. The weight of the farm, and its debts, caring for two small children, there wasn't much time for fooling around in barns, or fooling around anywhere for that matter. She missed the days when they had fun together. Perhaps it could be like that again. This thing with Jack was so exciting, but it wasn't real, and Sally knew it. It was true that he could turn her legs to jelly, and just the anticipation of seeing him gave her an adrenaline rush that could last all day, but he was married to someone else and they both knew this wasn't love but a way to recapture their quickly fading youth. To prove to herself she could still turn heads and that life wasn't all drudgery. Part of her wanted to run out of the hotel and get a cab all the way home. What had she gotten herself into, Bernard didn't deserve this and if he was to ever find out who knew what he might do. She pushed the thoughts out of her mind with a shudder and smoothed her hair down in the mirror before turning to go out and rejoin Jack at the bar.

It was then that she noticed Katie sitting at the other end of the bar, and the shock brought her up short. She was sitting with another woman who Sally had never seen before. She tried to ignore her friend and was going to walk out again when, with a lift of her eyebrows, Katie let Sally know that she had seen her. She didn't move or say a word but just turned her back as Sally rejoined Jack.

"Someone you know," Jack asked worriedly.

"Yes, but only vaguely don't worry about it." Sally dismissed his worries while trying to hide her own. She would have to speak to Katie later, but she wasn't sure how that conversation would go.

"Shall we take our drinks up to our room?" Jack suggested.

And Sally nodded in agreement; she was keen to get away from the eyes of her friend.

Their session together was not all Sally had hoped it would be because half the time she was thinking about Katie and what she was going to say. She knew that whatever she said, she came out of it looking like the bad guy. She just hoped she could trust Katie to keep her mouth shut. Katie had always had a soft spot for Bernard; they may have even dated back in school before Sally came on the scene. Katie had never mentioned it but she knew that they had always been close. Would she keep her secret or go running to Bernard in the hope he might turn to Katie for consolation? The reason Sally couldn't think of a way of spinning this was because she knew that whatever way you told it, she was in the wrong.

She tried to concentrate on Jack kissing her ears, but her mind wasn't on his foreplay. She pulled him on top of her. She needed to get this over and catch Katie before it was too late.

Jack dropped her at the edge of the village, and Sally reached the school gates just in time to pick Joshua up. Sally couldn't help but smile when she saw her youngest son, who had paint down the front of his uniform.

"Come on, sweet pea, we are going to make a stop at Auntie Katie's house for a little while," she said.

Joshua nodded; he loved Aunty Katie, who always made a fuss of him. Kate's house was only a few streets away from the school, and Sally was relieved to see Katie's car on the drive. Although, when she rang the bell and Katie answered the door, she could see that she didn't really want to speak to her.

"Can I come in?" Sally asked, walking into the hallway.

"Joshua, why don't you go out in the garden and play with Mr Tigggles?" Joshua went to the back door; he loved Katie's cat and was quite happy to go outside and find him.

Katie went into the kitchen, but she didn't put the kettle on, or ask Sally to sit down, like she usually would. Instead, she went back to chopping the vegetables she had been preparing.

"What do you want Sally?" she asked.

"I just didn't want you to get the wrong idea about what you saw at the hotel today."

"Right. What was it I saw?"

"Just me meeting up with an old friend. It didn't mean anything, but I would prefer if you didn't mention it to Bernard. You know how men can be."

"And when you went up to a hotel room with that old friend, I suppose that was innocent too, was it?"

"Keep your voice down. Joshua is just outside," Sally said, feeling panicky.

"I don't know how you have the nerve to come here and pretend there was nothing going on. You are unbelievable."

"Look Katie I thought we were friends. I just want to know that you are not going to tell Bernard."

"Get out, Sally, and take Joshua with you. I can't bear to look at you."

"Don't be like that; we are friends, Katie."

Sally went to move towards Katie in a gesture to try to appease her, but instead, knife still in hand, Katie turned and stood firm.

"Get out. And for the record, we have never been friends. I am Bernard's friend; remember, we have been friends since we were at school and you! Well, just get out."

Sally could hear the anger in her voice, and her stance told her she meant business. There was real aggression in her eyes as she clutched the knife. Visibly shaking, Sally went to the back door and called Joshua in; she shooed him out of the front door as quickly as she could.

On the way home, the scenario in the kitchen had Sally in an uneasy state of shock. Had Katie meant to threaten her with the knife? If Sally hadn't left straight away, would she have used the blade? She hadn't stayed to find out, but why was she so angry? Had Sally misjudged their friendship from the start? Perhaps Katie was in love with Bernard and only tolerated Sally to be around him, in which case this situation had played right into her hands. The scene at the hotel was running through her head. What was she going to do now? If she couldn't trust Katie to keep her mouth shut, she was in deep trouble. She couldn't bear the thought that Bernard would find out. Would he be violent? Would he track Jack down or just make her life a living hell? He might divorce her and try to take Joshua and Harry. Judges usually sided with the mother, but would they in this case? An unfaithful wife – well that didn't mean she was an unfit mother; lots of people had affairs. It did mean that she and the children might end up without a home. How could she afford to keep the children without Bernard? She had given up work when Joshua was born, and there were always things to do around the farm – running the farm shop, the accounts. Perhaps she would have to go back to work, and then there was childcare to consider, and the thoughts just kept running around and around her head.

It was then she made the fatal mistake of deciding to take the short cut across the cornfield. The footpath was the quickest way back to their house, and it looked like rain was threatening. Perhaps she was overreacting to the exchange in Katie's kitchen. Katie was bound to be a little upset; what she would do is wait until tomorrow, when Bernard was at work, and then call Katie again. By then she would have calmed down, and Sally could appeal to her and try to explain that if she did drop her bombshell, she would be breaking up their family. Yes, that would work. Ask her to think about the children and throw herself on Katie's mercy. Sally felt better already; now she had a plan. The rain started to fall in huge drops, and she pulled Joshua's hood up. "Will there be a rainbow, Mummy?" Sally laughed and bent down to do her son's coat up. "I think there will," were the last words she said.

Chapter 31
Sally's Background

The first thing Sally noticed about Bernard was his long legs in his faded jeans. Then she took in his short blonde hair. It was only when they made eye contact that she noticed his amazing blue eyes. They were very pale, a bit like a fish, she remembered thinking. He certainly didn't look like your average farmer. He was slim for a start, not stocky like most of the men propping up the bar of the Royal Oak. He was exceptionally tall as well, being at least 6ft 2". He looked like he would have been more at home on the pages of one of her glossy magazines rather than sitting astride his huge red tractor.

But it wasn't just his rugged good looks that attracted her, it was the way he listened to what she said and the way he made her laugh. She had stopped at the pub with her friend to break up the journey, and over her half of cider she had seen Bernard, and they had struck up a conversation. They had stayed at the pub for longer than they had expected; being surrounded by a group of attentive men had been fun, and when she left, she had bowed to Bernard's insistence that she give him her number. What the hell? You only live once, and he was very attractive. Within a few weeks they were an item, with him coming up to see her at her friend's house, and she was making a weekly trip down to the farm to stay with Bernard at his mum and dad's farm.

From the start, Sally loved the farm and the outdoor life. A city girl, she was keen to learn all about the animals and crops. She helped Bernard's mother with the baking and cooking; she was keen to get on well with all of Bernard's friends and was always willing to socialise down at the local pub. It didn't take Bernard long to realise she was the ideal partner. When the sheep gave birth, he couldn't wait to get on the phone and let Sally know about the new lambs, knowing she would be as excited as him, and when the harvest supper was planned, she was the first one he thought about inviting. Within a few months he was considering making this a full-time arrangement. He couldn't see the point of Sally living so far away when they could spend every day together under the same roof if she would become his wife. He was a practical kind of chap, and he realised that Sally would be a great help to his mother about the house and able to share his responsibilities on the farm. If not with the physical labour, she was good at bookkeeping and keeping his paperwork in order. And then, of course, there was the sex. Bernard was not a virgin and had fooled around with a few local girls, but there was no one like Sally. Sex with her was in another league. She knew exactly what to do to excite him, and she was always a willing partner. If he had thought about it at the time, he might have wondered about her past experiences in that area, as she seemed so knowledgeable. But he wasn't one to ponder on things, and why rock the boat when they had everything going for them?

Within the year they were married at the village church. It had never occurred to him that Sally wouldn't want to leave her job in the local shop and come and live on the farm. They were both keen to start a family straight away, and Sally fell pregnant almost at once. It was an exciting time, and all the family were glad for them, especially when Harry was born and then two years later little Joshua. He was the spitting image of his mother and had all her expressions and mannerism.

"He has you wrapped around his little finger." Sally would laugh.

"Just like his mother," he would reply. But it was true there was nothing he wouldn't do for the child. He often wondered if other parents felt so strongly for their children. In his eyes, he was absolutely perfect and could do no wrong. When Harry teased him, Bernard found himself getting really angry, and he knew just how to wind his brother up and then scream when he came anywhere near him. Childish squabbles Sally called it and told him to ignore their arguing.

"He loves the drama," she would say.

"Joshua is usually the instigator," she would explain to Bernard when he took Joshua's side, which was all of the time.

But he always felt that Harry was a bit heavy-handed with his younger brother, and sometimes his behaviour bordered on bullying. He couldn't understand why Sally just ignored it.

He tried to talk to his mum about it.

"Boys will be boys, and all children fight," she said.

"Sally's right, just ignore it."

Looking back, he wondered should he have done things differently. Should they have waited a while before starting a family and given themselves time to get to know each other first? Should he have delved more deeply into Sally's past? She always clammed up whenever he asked about her family and what she had done before she had met him.

"What difference does it make? I am here now. Let's just live in the here and now and forget about the past."

He had an uneasy feeling that perhaps he might have found out some things that he might not have liked if he had looked closer. And he did not want to spoil the perfect life they had. For it was perfect for the first few years. The babies were growing, the farm prospered, and all in all, he considered himself a very lucky man. He didn't know when he first noticed that Sally wasn't happy – was it straight after Joshua was born? Sally seemed moody and snapped at him when he questioned her about her bad temper. He put it down to postnatal depression, being stuck in doors a lot with the two children, and he had been worried enough to suggest she go along and see the doctor. But Sally had dismissed the suggestion. Then things had got slightly better, and he had stopped worrying or noticing her mood. He was busy on the farm and they opened the farm shop which Sally basically ran selling theirs and other local farm's produce. The following spring, his mother became poorly, and she and his dad decided to retire to a bungalow on the other side of the village and leave him and Sally to run the farm. It was true that the house was on the small side for four adults and two small children and although his parents loved their grandchildren, he wondered if living with them was proving too much for them. His mum continued to help out in the shop when she was needed. But on the day they moved out, he remembered feeling a deep sadness that they were going. This had been their home for decades, and in recent months there had been some cross words between Sally and his mother. He had never known them to argue before, but Sally was quick to take offence, and she said his mother was constantly criticising her. He tried not to take sides, but both women were obviously unhappy. He saw this as a new start for them all and hoped his parents would be happy in their new home. It also meant that he and Sally could have the place to themselves, and their growing family definitely needed that. Living on top of each other had not helped the situation, and he felt that once his parents were settled, then the relationship could be mended.

Chapter 32
The Mother-in-Law

From the moment I met Sally, I liked her, and I could see that Bernard, my son, liked her too. That was enough for me. He is my only son, and I wanted him to be happy. He worked hard on the farm, following in his Father's footsteps and all he wanted, as a child, was to leave school and work alongside his father. He had a great love for the land, and although farming can be a hard life, it can also be rewarding.

Bernard didn't have much time for women, as he worked long hours, and not every girl is happy with that. From the start, Sally showed that she was willing to muck in and help out. She embraced the life and, even though she came from the city, she was willing to learn new things and work hard.

I grew to love her like a daughter, but there was always something about her. Like an emptiness that she was trying to fill. For instance, she never spoke about her parents. It was as though she was so willing to become one of our family because she didn't have one of her own. I am not sure how true that is, but she never spoke about her past, her childhood, where she went to school, her friends, or jobs she had. Instead, she lived solely in the present. This is not a bad thing, just slightly unusual, and it could be unnerving. For instance, when we went shopping for Harry's first school uniform we went into town and made a day of it. We had lunch, bought the uniform, from the uniform shop, and little Harry looked so grown up in it.

"Do you remember your first day at school?" I asked her.

A cloud crossed her face like she was remembering something awful, and then her expression changed, and she said, "No, that was a long time ago."

I said I remembered my first day at school, and I had been a little nervous, but I had made lots of new friends, and I was sure Harry would do the same.

"Of course he will," she said, smiling at him. "He already knows lots of children from nursery."

But she seemed cross with me for bringing up her past and hardly spoke all the way home.

Chapter 33
Who Was Sally?

There are lots of things about Sally that I never knew. She had been married before, for instance, a fact she kept very quiet. I never thought I was the first man she had loved, but I did think I was the only man she had married, but it would seem not. Not if the marriage certificate I found squirrelled away is true, and I have no reason to doubt that it is. She was married when she was nineteen to a guy called James when she lived in London. In the small storage box that contained her marriage certificate, there was also a decree nisi, so at least I know she was legally my wife, and the box also contained some jewellery and pictures of Sally with long, dark locks. At first, I didn't recognise her, but the back showed dates, names and so it would seem it was her. I had only ever known her as a blonde, and in my naivety, I had always thought she was naturally that colour; perhaps she was, and the black was a dye that she used back then. In the photos, she had a wanton look with revealing clothes and sexy poses. Well, perhaps she was different when she was younger not the poised, sophisticated woman I had met at twenty-five.

There were swimming certificates and letters, tied in a red bow, which I could not bring myself to read. A past love affair – my heart was already broken, and I didn't know how much more I could take. I began to wonder if she had another child with this man, James, and whether if I went back to the address I found for her mother there would be a host of other secrets that she had chosen to keep from me and her new family. Who knows what she was running away from, but in all the time we had been together, there had been no contact with the people who raised her or friends from those bygone days. She had been very careful to cover her tracks, which made me wonder what she was hiding from.

When she had been taken, I had considered getting in touch with her family, but part of me was frightened. The girl I saw in the photos was nothing like the woman I was married to, and I wondered what I would find out. Finally, the idea had faded, but after all the publicity, I was sure someone would come forward, but it had never happened. Now, having found this box at the back of her wardrobe, I had the information I needed to contact her mother if I wanted and find out more about Sally's life before I met her. Surely I owed it to her family to let them know that she was gone, and was it right to deny Harry access to his maternal grandparents?

Chapter 34
Sally's Story

I was always a little wild, even as a child. "She has no fear," my mother used to say. What she meant was I was always getting into scrapes and trying things I shouldn't, climbing that tree in a neighbour's garden, skateboarding in the park with the bigger kids, fighting with other girls over a packet of cigarettes in the playground after school. I suppose I never thought the rules applied to me.

My father was a shady figure who came and went throughout my childhood. When he left, he usually took the money out of mum's purse and her bill money; behind him, he usually left mum with a black eye or marks that she had to keep covered up for week. As I got older, we spent a lot of time hiding from him in women's refuges or friends' homes, but it taught me to rely only on myself. Mum had an army of female friends, most of whom were in the same position as us – too little money and husbands or partners who were rough or violent. But looking after yourself can be hard work, and it was no surprise when, as a teenager, I found a man who I thought would be my saviour. I was happy to marry him and escape the drudgery I saw all around me, but it turned out I swapped one bad situation for another.

James, or Jimmy to his friends, was a drug dealer and

a violent one at that, and it didn't take me long to realise that a life with him was going to be ten times worse than it had been living at home. Had I been so naive that I had chosen the same sort of man as my mother had married? What I thought was strength turned out to be a need to control. His jealousy and temper were always ready to flare up and sometimes his unpredictable behaviour left me fearing for my life. So, I left. With the help of my mum and her army of friends, I made a clean break away from the city, somewhere no one would find me.

One of my 'aunties' had a niece, who lived in the country near the South Coast, and she was willing to help me get set up down there. So I dyed my hair blonde, took the minimum of belongings, and moved on with my life. I was a new me.

Later I filed for divorce, and by that time Jimmy had another partner and kids in tow and didn't really care. I was replaceable. He had been angry that I had left, but he soon found someone to take my place, and he didn't contest the divorce. By then I had met Bernard, and my real life had begun. I think I loved him in a way I had never loved anyone before, and when I had the children, I was determined to give them the childhood I had never known.

So I threw myself into the life on the farm with his parents, who were very good to me, and for a long time everything was wonderful. But that wildness that was in my soul never really went away. I loved being out in the fresh air and taking the children to the beach or just making picnics in the garden, but I started to feel that there was nothing that was just for me. I was a good wife, mother and daughter-in-law, but amongst all these roles I played, where was the wild child I had once been, and so when I saw Jack that day, I thought this could be something just for me. He was my guilty pleasure, but even with him, I felt sometimes that I was playing the role of the other woman. The connection between us was tenuous. It was never the way I felt about Bernard. He was my mate for life; Jack was the adrenalin-fuelled excitement that I needed – a quick fix.

Life at the farm had started to tear at my nerves. I felt like my mother-in-law, Angela, was always finding fault with the way I did things, especially how I was bringing up the children. So, when my in-laws moved out, life became easier in a way; I was my own woman, doing things my way, but things were harder too. More work to do on the farm, not so much help with the children, and the farm shop to run sometimes on my own. It had been what I wanted, but when they had gone, I missed them. And part of me felt like I had failed; failed at being part of a family. For this was the family I had never had. They had let me into their home, and I had driven them away. The sadness would wash over me in waves,+ and Bernard was oblivious.

Chapter 35
First Meeting

Jack had just popped into the post office to buy a sandwich for lunch when his eyes made contact with Sally. She was beautiful in a rangy way – tall, slender in bright wellies and an Aran sweater. He had a glimpse of her between the aisles and was overwhelmed with a physical attraction and so he hung back until he saw her take her basket to the counter. He made sure he looked directly at her and made it clear that he was interested, because he was. It had been a bad morning. The client he had been to visit had been an established customer, so he was expected a chat to keep him sweet and perhaps to take him out to lunch in a nearby pub. Instead, he had been greeted by a barrage of complaints about his latest order and the news that he would no longer be putting any work their way. Jack tried to talk him round, but he realised it wasn't going to work, and he knew that the man was in no mood to be placated. All he could do was beat a hasty retreat, hence the need for a sandwich. He wasn't looking forward to returning to the office and Lydia's anger and snide comments. Not racking up any new customers this month was one thing, but losing one who had traded with them for years was another.

She needed to realise it was hard to sell the service when the warehouse kept messing orders up. But his wife took no prisoners; she was determined to make a success of the business her father entrusted to her. He understood that James, Lydia's father, was always taking her to task for lost opportunities and questioning the way she ran the business, but sometimes Jack felt like he was just an employee, and a lowly one at that, rather than her husband.

So he had made idle chitchat at the till with Sally, and it boosted his ego to see that this lovely young woman found him attractive too. It wasn't long before they had swapped mobile numbers, discreetly, of course, after they had finished their shopping. So, he had called her and started to text her when he was in the area and even when he wasn't. It wasn't as though he hadn't done this before, but since he had married the boss's daughter, he had to be more careful. No juvenile banter in the office about his latest conquests or sneaky telephone calls in the apartment he shared with Lydia in the earlier days. No, now he was very discreet. After all, he had a cushy number with Lydia. It was true she had all the money and held the reins in their relationship. But that was okay by him; he was never going to be an amazing salesman, he was quite happy to coast and let his wife pick up the tab for his lavish lifestyle. He drove an expensive car, had a beautiful home in a good part of town, and overall life was going well. Could he help it if he had always been a bit greedy and wanted more? And at that moment he wanted Sally, and he didn't see why he couldn't have her. It turned out she was more than willing, and she knew the score. She was married herself and didn't want to get found out either. The situation suited both of them – an affair with all the excitement that would bring with none of the hassle.

It was true that when he realised she had children, he had a moment of guilt. He and Lydia had decided to leave parenting until later, and he had always thought that once he was a dad he would stop his philandering. If he really thought about it, he did not feel like an adult at all. All he was doing was having fun while he could, and he knew one day he would have to start to take his responsibilities seriously. But if she wasn't worried about the consequences of their sexual encounters, why should he? After all, she had the most to lose. But it did make him more mindful of their situation; no one wanted the mess that discovery would doubtlessly lead to. That was why when they booked a room, he always paid with cash, and their lunches were at places way out of town.

He liked to treat her with presents and trinkets; wasn't that what a lover was supposed to do? He played his part well, and he was well rewarded. If they didn't love one another, they certainly enjoyed each other's company, and it even spiced up his own sex life with Lydia.

After the lunchtime session at the hotel, he had left the village feeling pleased with himself. Just one or two calls before his return home. He picked up a bottle of wine at the off licence on the way. Lydia was home before him and was cooking a spaghetti. He hadn't eaten much at lunchtime, as he didn't want to feel bloated and impede his performance. But now he had worked up an appetite and was looking forward to a good home-cooked meal.

"Darling, I am home," he called as he turned his key in the lock.

"You look like you have had a good day," Lydia replied as she turned from the cooker and saw his smile.

Chapter 36
The Aftermath

It wasn't until about four days later that Jack started to panic. When he hadn't heard from Sally for a couple of days, he was confused, and then he began to worry. It wasn't like her to stay silent for so long. There must be a problem. He wracked his brain about what had happened at the hotel. Had he done something wrong? No, as far as he knew, they had left on good terms. In fact, they had a great afternoon. Perhaps she was ill or in hospital and could not use her phone. He made sure the texts he sent her were bland and did not compromise her in any way. It might be that her husband was monitoring her calls. A sort of dread started to move through him. What if her husband knew? What would he do?

He wondered if he was the jealous type, and Jack began to realise that neither of them had spoken much about their partners. All he knew was that the husband was a local farmer and that Sally had married him young and had two small children. He knew that it suited him not to ask questions about her marriage, as his own did not bear looking at. He had given her the minimum of information about his wife and home. The last thing he wanted was Sally turning up at his front door. So it suited them both to live in a bubble when they were together and forget the outside world. Only now he realised that contacting Sally if she didn't answer his texts was a problem. He thought about calling her but was worried that her husband might answer if Sally wasn't well.

He resorted to the internet to find out about local farms in her area, and he remembered the farm shop he had once visited. Neither of these pieces of information seemed to throw up anything, so he typed in her name. The shock was overwhelming. Sally's face came up a smiling image of her and her young son, but the headline was what had him running to be sick in the downstairs toilet. He didn't have time to read the detail.

Since then, Jack had found himself with so many emotions. They seemed to swing like a pendulum; one minute he was hyper-alert, feeling that he must be careful in anything he said. Then a feeling of deep sorrow would wash over him as he thought of their last time together, her infectious laugh, and the lingering kisses. He felt that Sally had really known him, as they seemed so alike deep down. Finally, he was scared, in a way he had never been frightened before. His whole life was hanging by a thread; if Lydia found out, it would be the last straw, and the police might come knocking at his door at any moment. He felt like he was going mad. Over and over he would relive their time together and try to remember where they had been, who had seen them and might report this to the Police, and if anything suspicious had happened to make him think Sally might be in any danger.

Chapter 37
The Station

As Pete sat on the bench at the draughty station, he saw the train on the other platform approaching. The barriers across the road went down, halting the traffic to a standstill. The passengers disembarked, and the train pulled out of the station. The delay of his train meant he had almost an hour to wait. He sighed with exasperation, and then he noticed Bernard with his luggage, putting his ticket in his coat pocket, on the opposite platform.

"Hi, Pete, how long have you got to wait?"

"About an hour there is a problem further up the line."

"Do you fancy a coffee?"

"Well okay," Pete didn't know what to say; in all the time he had known Bernard, he had never really initiated any contact or friendliness. Of course they acknowledged each other, but he was always busy on the farm, and they hardly knew each other. But what could he say? The man had lost his wife, and Pete had been one of her friends.

"Do you mind if we have it here, as I don't want to miss the train?"

"I'll come across the bridge."

They both made their way to the station cafe and put in their orders.

"Have you been to London?"

"Yes, the police have a national investigation going on, and they wanted me to look at some photographs."

"Did you recognise anyone?"

"No. But it wasn't a total waste of time."

"Oh?"

"Well, they brought me up to speed on what they are doing and the links between Sally's murder and that of May Greene."

"Are they linking the murders rather than looking at them individually?"

"Yes, they seem to think that this man is preying on women across the country."

It occurred to Pete that Bernard had not mentioned his son's murder.

"I just wanted to say how sorry I am about Sally and little Joshua."

Bernard brushed this aside as if he couldn't bear to think of his tiny son.

"Thanks, Pete. It is difficult to talk about it with anyone. My parents and Harry are devasted, and I can't talk about the police investigation at home in case I upset them. And it is not as if you can just pop into the local pub and start up a conversation about such a terrible topic."

"I understand Bernard."

"And how are you holding up?" The look on his face said everything.

"Silly question, really. I can't imagine what you are going through. If there is anything I can do please let me know."

"Where are you off to?" Bernard asked. Pete found

himself feeling guilty as if he was running away, which he was.

"Oh, I am just going to quote for some work over at Farnham." Bernard looked down at his suitcase.

"I thought I might stay overnight."

They finished their coffees, and it was when they went out to the platform and said their goodbyes that the police officer approached, and Bernard and Pete both looked at each other wondering which one of them they wanted.

"Mr Peter Douglas, we wondered if you could come into the station and answer a few questions, please."

"I was just on my way to Farnham."

"It would be much appreciated if you could assist us straight away," the police officer said.

"Okay," Pete replied, he did not want to sound churlish. Bernard was looking at him with suspicion.

"We have a car waiting outside." The officer led him through the station. It was one of the longest and most embarrassing walks of his life. He felt as if everyone was looking at him and whispering. Was he a suspect?

Chapter 38
In Custody

If the train had not been delayed, I would have got away, he remembered thinking as they led him to the police car and stowed his luggage in the boot. He supposed it looked suspicious to be leaving town in the middle of an investigation. They led him into an interview room and asked him to take a seat. Pete had never been inside a police station, let alone an interview room, but it was just like he had seen on the TV. He wondered if he would be spending the night in a cell and he felt frightened.

"I understand that you were close with Sally Armstrong, Mr Douglas."

The officer wasted no time in getting straight to the point.

"I wouldn't say that. I knew her and her kids attended a lot of clubs that my children do."

"Like?"

"Well, the swimming club and the gymnastics."

The officer made a note in his notebook. "Right. And you were on the PTA and a number of committees together."

"Yes."

"So you were close acquaintances."

"As I said, not really close."

"Did she confide in you?"

"No, she had lots of friends at the school; you know, other mothers who she chatted with all the time, I am sure they could be of more help to you."

"That's funny because a lot of the ladies at the school say you two were especially close, often out for coffee, whispering in corners, laughing and joking," the officer added.

"Well, Officer, you know what school playgrounds are like."

"No, I don't actually, Mr Douglas; why don't you tell me what they are like?" Officer Jackson replied.

"Well, women like to gossip, and a man and a woman being friends is a juicy subject."

"So you were friends, or were you more than that, Mr Douglas."

"No. We were not in a relationship if that is what you mean, Officer Jackson."

"But did she tell you things, perhaps about her marriage? Was it a happy marriage, for instance?"

"I don't know."

"She never spoke about her husband or you about your wife?"

"No."

"You are a landscape gardener, aren't you, Mr Douglas, and you have a lot of time to ferry the children around while your wife works full time. Is that right?"

"Yes, I suppose so. I can set my hours to suit myself and my family."

"How many children do you have?"

"Four."

"Not much time to spend with your wife with her working full time and you looking after the four children, and Sally Armstrong was a very attractive woman."

"What are you getting at?"

"Were you having an affair with Sally Armstrong?"

"No. I have already told you we were not in a relationship."

"Would it surprise you to hear that many people at the school thought you were?"

"Well, they would be wrong."

"When was the last time you saw Sally Armstrong, Mr Douglas?"

Pete considered lying and then reconsidered, "I think it was outside the Coop about a week before she died."

"What did you talk about?"

"We just exchanged pleasantries and passed the time of day. You know, hello, how are you?"

"And how was she?"

"Fine."

"Did you argue?"

"No."

"Then why did she tell you to 'Piss Off'."

"She didn't."

"I have a witness who says she heard Sally tell you to 'Piss Off' and then she got in her car and sped off. Are you sure you didn't continue that conversation at a later date, or perhaps you confronted her about whatever she was angry about in the cornfield?"

"I think I need to have a solicitor present if you are

going to question me further."

"That is your right, Mr Douglas, but you are only helping us with our enquiries at the moment."

"Even so, I feel that I do not want to say any more without legal representation."

"Okay Mr Douglas do you have a solicitor, or would you like me to call the duty solicitor?"

"The duty solicitor, please."

The officer left Pete sitting in the dark station room. "What was he going to do now?"

Chapter 39
The Investigation Picks up Speed

The inspector was making his way down to Sussex after a development in the Joshua and Sally Armstrong murders. They had a suspect in custody, a local man who had been friends with the family and who had been seen arguing with Sally a week before the murder. One of his officers had been questioning the man, but the inspector wanted to be on the spot and make sure the interviews were handled properly.

There were also some other leads. There was a member of the bar staff at a local hotel who had remembered seeing a woman matching Sally's description on the day of the murder. The local police had been retracing her footsteps in greater detail, and this woman had come forward with what she recollected from the day. She seemed to be a reliable witness, and although she did not previously know Sally, she had looked at the photographs in the local paper, and she thought the woman she had seen could have been her. The woman had been in the bar with a man, who the bar person thought was probably a Londoner – by his accent and clothes. This mystery man intrigued the inspector there had been no mention of any discord between the Armstrong's up until this point. So first he needed to establish if the woman in the bar was Sally and then, if so, who was the man she was drinking with. He hadn't dismissed Bernard's suspicion about the immigrant worker, Ahmed, either. He wanted to talk to the farmer who had employed Ahmed when he had worked on his farm and see if he had an alibi for the day of the murder. As the inspector went back through the folder of evidence, he tried to keep it separate from the other murders that had taken place in the vicinity; after all, May Greene had been killed by a totally different MO, but he also recognised that three such violent deaths so close to each other could not be total coincidence; something was niggling him. If there was a murderer in this area, why had he not struck again since the last murder? It had been a few months now. If Bernard was right, perhaps it was because the refugee had moved to London and it was taking him time to find his way around. Having settled into his new surroundings, could it be that Ahmed was planning to continue his killing spree when he approached the young mother, and her child in the sandpit?

There were many loose ends in this case, and the inspector wanted to revisit the murder site to see if it gave him a sense of the murderer's motivation. One of the positives the post-mortem on both victims had established was that neither of the women had been sexually assaulted, but in the case of Sally Armstrong, there was evidence of sexual intercourse a few hours prior to the attack. It would be interesting to see if this timeline coincided with her visit to the Hotel. Of course, it could have been that she had sex with her husband that morning, and that could be established with a simple DNA test from Bernard. But what if this wasn't the case? How difficult was it going to be for the young widower to learn his dead wife had been unfaithful on the day she died?

Well, it was a murder case, and if it led to the apprehension of the killer, and if Sally's last sexual partner turned out to be her murderer, then they must follow the evidence wherever it led.

Flicking through the rest of the file, the inspector started to think of the murder weapon. It had never been recovered. But there had been plenty of time to dispose of it and any bloody clothes. As time moved on, its recovery was unlikely unless they had a stroke of luck.

Chapter 40
Running Away

Jack's hands felt clammy, and his anxiety was lurking just below the surface. Every time the buzzer went, he thought Lydia was going to announce the police had arrived to speak to him. In his darkest moments, he knew it was only a matter of time before they found out about the affair and tracked him down. When he was feeling more optimistic, he thought that perhaps he had been lucky and got away with it – that no one, including his wife, would know. One thing he knew he was going to be much more careful in future; he had a lot to lose and now he was just beginning to appreciate the life he had with Lydia. What had he been thinking chasing women all over the country? Did he really think he could get away with it forever? He had not foreseen what happened to poor Sally, but he was bound to get found out at some stage; he had just never imagined it would be in such a dramatic fashion.

At home he was bounding between being super attentive to his wife and sitting morosely hearing nothing that was being said to him.

"Are you okay, Jack," Lydia had asked the night before, after he had sat for a good fifteen minutes staring blankly out of the bi-fold doors into the black sky.

"What!" He was totally unaware of what she had been

saying.

"Is something wrong?"

"No. Nothing."

"You have been acting strangely for the last few days; like you are on another planet. I was just asking if you had a sales trip booked for April."

Jack shrugged and tried to keep a lid on his aggravation.

"Can't we just have one evening at home when we don't talk about business. I am fed up of being questioned about my every move. I will let you know when I am going to be away from home. But for now, can we just be husband and wife relaxing in our own living room and not boss and employee?"

Lydia looked hurt.

"I didn't mean to question your movements. I wondered if you wanted to go away for a few days and if you could fit it into your schedule. A little rest and relaxation would do us both good."

"Have you okayed, it with your father? Can he spare you?" Jack said, sarcasm dripping from each word.

"What's got into you, Jack? You know it is always better to plan holidays before the staff want to be off in high season."

Jack felt the tension in the back of his neck and shoulders intensify. At that moment, he could have literally strangled Lydia, she was being so annoying. He was beginning to think that the price he had to pay for all the luxuries he had always craved was just too high if he had to put up with her whining. Then it occurred to him that a trip out of the country might be just what he needed. It would mean that the police would find it harder to contact him, and when all the media activity had calmed down, he could come back. Once he had decided it was safe.

He changed his scowl into a smile. "Do you know, darling, that is not a bad idea? Why don't you go ahead and look on the computer for somewhere hot and far away? Let's treat ourselves to a break somewhere exotic; we both deserve it."

She crossed the room and rubbed his shoulders. "You could do with some relaxation and sunshine."

"Yes, let's make it a longer trip this year – what about two or even three weeks? We could ask James to cover. He would like that."

The idea of letting her younger brother run the business, even for a short time, made Lydia apprehensive, but then she looked at Jack. They did need some time together away from the office. Over the last few months, she felt they had been drifting apart. Perhaps now was the time to put her relationship first.

"Okay," she said. "Where do you fancy?"

Chapter 41
The Lover

Katie held her breathe and submerged her head under the water. The bath was hot and fragrant, but as she came up for air, she could not feel the relaxation she had envisaged when she had taken sanctuary in her bathroom. Her mind was still buzzing with the thoughts that had been going through her head since she had met up with Bernard in the village. From the moment they had seen each other across the road, she had felt on edge, and when he had crossed over to speak to her, the conversation between them had been stilted and filled with awkward gaps. She had tried to be as normal as possible so that he did not suspect how nervous she was feeling and the alarm she had felt ever since she had heard of Sally's death. Whether she had played a part or been the person to actually kill Sally played on a rerunning loop inside her head. But it wasn't until she had struggled over a few sentences that she realised that he was finding the conversation as difficult as she was. He seemed vague and distant, not something that should seem unusual after what he had been through, and she could put it down to grief, shock and a whole host of emotions on that spectrum. If it was not for a nagging feeling that he seemed frightened – frightened of saying something that would incriminate him – that would give too much away. It struck her that he was playing the part of the grieving husband rather than being sad. She recognised this because she was playing a similar role as the grieving friend. Neither of them seemed to be able to meet each other's eyes as he told her about his trip to London to help the police with their enquiries, and she asked if there were any leads.

"Not that they have shared with me," he had said with a shake of his head.

Now as she lay in the bath, his next words came back to her.

"Perhaps we will never know what happened to Sally. Maybe we didn't know the real Sally at all."

At the time this had seemed like a strange thing to say, but now as Katie turned it over in her mind, she wondered if Bernard had known that Sally was having an affair, or perhaps he had just suspected. All those years she had watched their marriage and been envious; perhaps she had the wrong idea, and it was not as perfect as she had thought. Maybe she should have acted on her feelings and told him how she felt. She had been so scared of being rejected and frightened that she would be seen as a home wrecker that she had never shown her real feelings. She was afraid of being seen as a sad lonely woman, who was obsessed with a man who did not want her. But now Bernard was all alone with his little boy, and there might be a chance for them to rekindle what they once had. Katie began to scrub herself vigorously. It was no good worrying about what happened when she passed out. She had tried to rack her brain for memories of after Sally left the house that day, to no avail. The amount she had drunk was enough, she felt, to make her blackout seem plausible, and until someone else questioned what had happened, she would just keep quiet and help Bernard get over his loss. If this led to stronger feelings on both their parts, well, that was an outcome no one could have foreseen.

But if Bernard did know about Sally's affair, did that mean he might have killed her? Did he have it in him to murder his wife and small child? Katie dismissed this out of hand. Even if he'd known and wanted to kill Sally, he could never have hurt Joshua, she told herself. So if she did not do it, and Bernard had not done it that left a stranger or the elusive lover. What did he have to lose? Was he married, and did he even know that Sally was dead?

Whatever way you looked at it, Bernard would not thank her for telling him his dead wife had an affair. But what if the lover was the murderer? If Katie could not tell Bernard about the lover, should she tell the police? NO, why bring herself to the attention of the police and risk Bernard finding out she had known about the affair? Why not make her own enquiries and find out who this man was and make up her own mind as to whether he was the murderer?

A plan was forming in Katie's head, and it all led back to the morning she had seen Sally at the hotel. Someone there must know something, and she was going to find out what. She climbed out of the bath, slipped on her dressing gown and went to get her telephone. Then she rang the hotel and made a reservation for lunch. It would be quite easy to talk to the staff in an informal way about the last time Sally visited. The whole area was talking about the murder and people loved to gossip.

Katie's enquiries at the hotel had borne fruit. One of the chambermaids remembered Sally and her lover. She said they had been in the hotel on a number of occasions; she remembered the white Audi that the man drove, and she said she was sure that when you check in, you have to register the number plate to park in the car park. Katie had said she would pay good money for that number, and the girl was happy to take the cash and furnish Katie with the details she wanted. It had been that simple. Katie was then able to trace the number plate and find out the address of the owner of the car. With the information at her fingertips, she was beginning to get cold feet. What was she going to say to this man, and was she putting herself in danger in approaching him? Should she just turn what she knew over to the police.

But finally, she decided to take the matter in her own hands and took the trip to the city where Jack Harris lived. He had a smart but modest house in the suburbs, an upgrade from the apartment he had originally shared with Lydia. Having watched the house for a number of hours, Katie saw his wife, or partner, leave for work and seeing his car still in the drive, she guessed that he was at home alone. Katie rang the doorbell and explained that she was a friend of Sally's. At first he started to deny knowing anyone by that name. When Katie insisted she knew he had been having a relationship with Sally, he invited her into the house, and once inside the house he did have the decency to look shamefaced. The room was immaculate, and he gestured for Katie to sit on the sofa. It was true he said he had known Sally and he had seen what had happened to her in the paper.

"I only have a few minutes I have to get to work," Jack blustered.

Katie got straight to the point. "Didn't you think it was your duty to come forward and say you were with Sally on the day of the murder?" Katie asked.

"What good would that do? I didn't do it, and it happened after she left me. All that would achieve would be my wife would find out and Sally's husband would be even more unhappy."

"Glad you were thinking of Sally's husband in all this and not just yourself."

Jack sat down opposite Katie. "Have you been to the police with what you know?" Jack asked sheepishly.

"Not yet. I wanted to meet you first and see what you had to say for yourself."

"Well, I swear to you I had nothing to do with the murder. I think the Police are looking into the idea that it was a stranger to the area. Someone Sally didn't even know. There was that woman on her bicycle as well a week later."

"Yes, I know, but that doesn't let you off the hook. The police might want to rule you out of their enquiries."

"Can you please not tell the police. You don't know how much damage you would do, and for what? It would just detract from their main lines of enquiry."

"What you mean is it will leave you in the frame."

"Yes. I suppose you could say that. But I am begging

you, please just forget what you know."

Katie stood up and walked to the door. "Look, let's not be hasty. I could make it worth your while to keep quiet about what you saw. It was an affair, yes, but I can assure you I didn't hurt your friend. I loved her." A sob escaped from Jack's lips as the realisation for the first time that his feelings for Sally had run deeper than he had thought.

"I haven't decided what I am going to do," Katie said as she walked back to the front door.

"I will let you know when I have decided," she exited, slamming the door behind her.

Jack was left feeling frightened and shaken. What now? Well, if this woman didn't accept his offer of money, more drastic measures might have to be taken.

Chapter 42
The Interview

Up in London, the inspector decided to send a plain clothes constable to the hospital again, where Ahmed worked, and see if he had turned up yet. Perhaps the uniformed officer had made Ahmed nervous, and so this time he would play it low-key, and if that didn't work, they would have to visit him at home. Although they had nothing to go on except the hunch of the husband, the inspector did not feel he could ignore this lead even if it came to nothing. This case was proving tricky. There were no witnesses and little DNA evidence. Whoever committed these crimes had been careful enough to cover their tracks. No murder weapon had been found, and somewhere out there was a murderer who was hiding himself and the axe he had used.

The forensic evidence wasn't making any sense. Sally and Joshua's murders seemed to be a crime of aggression and violence, and May's murder had a different feel like an execution – planned and organised. The first murder was a frenzied attack with an axe, and the second a quick execution with a knife. And yet the local police believed that they were linked. Of course both crimes took place in the same area over a brief period of time, but there was more to it than that. On his train journey down to Sussex, he reviewed all the details of the case just in case he had missed anything. He was keen to get to the station and find out what the man they had taken in for questioning had to say.

"How long has he been held?" the inspector asked as he entered the room.

"Only a couple of hours, but he is refusing to talk without a solicitor."

"And."

"The duty solicitor is on her way."

"What do you think?"

"Difficult to judge this one; he is certainly hiding something, but I don't know if he is capable of killing someone so violently. He is a landscape gardener."

The inspector gave Officer Jackson a hard look. "You would be amazed what people are capable of when pushed to breaking point. Landscape gardener or not."

"Any form."

"No, sir. A law abiding citizen."

"Until now."

"Okay, let's play this like he is helping us to solve the murder of his friend, and anything he can tell us will be useful."

"He is lying about the last time he saw her. He denies that she told him to piss off."

"Right, so you come in hard about that, and I will go softly, softly. Let me know when the Duty Solicitor arrives and get me any information we have: his wife, kids, and the reliability of the witness who heard him with Sally."

"Yes, sir." Jackson set about printing off his notes for the inspector, who went to get himself a cup of the station's disgusting coffee.

"Good afternoon, Mr Douglas." The inspector nodded at the solicitor who was now sitting with her client.

"We want to thank you for coming in to help with our enquiries. I know you and Sally Armstrong were close, and like you, we want to see the man who did this terrible thing brought to justice."

Pete felt himself to be under pressure; where was this leading? He was very much on his guard.

"Yes," he managed to answer.

"Can you tell me where you were on the day of the murder?"

Pete outlined the jobs he had been working on that day and explained to the inspector that there were several clients who could vouch for his whereabouts.

"Don't worry about that now. I will have one of my officers verify your alibi later."

"Am I right in thinking then, inspector, that my client is a suspect for the murder of Sally Armstrong?"

"Well, I suppose that depends on how this interview goes and how honest your client decides to be about his relationship with the deceased."

"I had nothing to do with her murder," Pete volunteered.

"That may be so, but you lied about your meeting outside the co-op, and that leads us to believe you are hiding something," Officer Jackson interrupted.

The solicitor looked at Pete before continuing.

"May I speak to my client alone," she asked.

"Make it quick we have a murderer to find." Officer

Jackson quipped as he and the inspector left the room.

Ten minutes later, they were back in the room, seated in the same places.

"Well?" the inspector asked.

"My client is willing to tell you what he knows, but he wants assurances that whatever he tells you is confidential."

"I am sorry I can't make any promises; this is a murder investigation, and any parts of your statement may be used in court, Mr Douglas. Do you understand how serious this is? Withholding evidence is a serious offence."

Pete shook his head. "Then I have nothing to say."

"Well then, I am afraid you will be spending some time in a cell while you think about it."

"Are you charging my client?"

"Not yet. Just giving him time to think about the consequences of not co-operating with us."

"Take him back to the cells," the inspector told the officer outside the door.

Chapter 43
Options

Back in London, Ahmed was considering his options. He had finally returned to his own flat, as the lies about the rat exterminator could not be carried on forever. He had enjoyed his time at Rachael's place. And having been there over two weeks and having consummated their relationship, he was in no hurry to go home. He had called in sick at work, and since returning to the area, he had checked out whether the hospital was being watched. He was almost sure that it wasn't and that it was safe to return to work. He did not want to run away again. He had a steady job and a relationship with a girl he was fond of, and starting all over again seemed like hard work. Perhaps the police had forgotten about him, he thought optimistically.

He had managed to elude them for so long that perhaps they thought he had moved on. Having spent the day at work and enjoying the routine after being absent for a while, it was a surprise then when two plain clothes officers had turned up at his flat that very evening as he was eating his tea. Having been on the run for so long, his apprehension was very low-key. He went along meekly with no fuss or complaining. He felt like this moment had always been inevitable from the start, and all his travelling and hiding were just a way of putting off this time that was always going to arrive. He talked to the officers on the way into the station and said he was happy to answer any questions they had.

Once in custody, he confessed to the murders while the police taped his confessions and made notes on a large pad of some of the details he was willing to impart. Later, they gave him tea and toast while he waited in the cell for the inspector to arrive and the charges to be brought. He wasn't impatient or frightened; this was what he had always expected to happen, and although he had tried to avoid this outcome, part of him was relieved that he could finally be honest and face the consequences. The officers on the case listened carefully and asked follow-up questions, but they were not violent or unkind. This surprised him as his only dealings with the police or army in his own country, although few had left a bad aftertaste as they were violent and dangerous.

It had taken a good few hours to get the crimes on tape and down on paper, and they were very interested in the whereabouts of the murder weapons. Although he could tell them about burning the clothes he had been wearing during the murders of Joshua and Sally, he pretended he could not recollect what he had done with the axe and knife he had used. This was mainly because he did not want to get the farmer he had worked for in trouble. He had been good to him, and he did not see why they needed to involve him if they had a confession.

It seemed the police would want to take a DNA sample from him once he was charged, and this would be matched to evidence, they had from the bodies. Ahmed told them he had no objection to this.

Chapter 44
Pete is Questioned

Back in Sussex, after hours in the cell, and with advice from his solicitor, Pete had finally decided to co-operate.

"It wasn't what you might think," he started.

"Sally and I were just friends, and I had nothing to do with what happened to her. It was just a misunderstanding outside the co-op."

"A misunderstanding?" the inspector asked.

"I had seen Sally with a man at the farm shop a few days before, and I was just teasing her about it."

"What do you mean when you say you saw her with a man? Surely lots of men visit the farm shop. What were they doing exactly?"

"Let's say they were fooling around."

"Were they kissing, having sex, be specific."

"I don't know, but I had obviously interrupted them."

"Where were they?"

"In the back room."

"Did you see the man, and did you know him?"

"No."

"So, he wasn't local."

"I don't think so. I didn't actually see him. I could hear they were busy, and so I made a swift exit."

"And why didn't you think to mention this when Sally

and Joshua were murdered?"

"I didn't want to get involved."

"You do know that withholding evidence in a murder enquiry could lead to you being prosecuted and imprisoned."

Pete went pale. "I didn't think it was important."

"You didn't think it was important, or you didn't want to get involved? The two are very different. Did you threaten to tell Sally's husband?"

Pete looked at his solicitor, who nodded.

"I might have."

"And is that why there was this altercation outside the Co-op? You had better think very carefully, Mr Douglas. Is there anything else you need to tell me?"

"I don't think so."

"Do you have any objections to us taking a DNA sample just to eliminate you from our enquiries."

"No, if you think it will help."

"Well, the officer will take you back to the cells for a while, and then someone will come and take your DNA. I want you to think about what the man said and about his voice, and the officer will take these details down. After that, we will talk again."

"Does my wife need to hear about this?" Pete asked as they led him out.

"That depends where this leads," the inspector replied.

Chapter 45
Life Goes On

Bernard's meeting with Katie was playing on his mind too. Even though they had been friends since they were children, he felt an unease between them. Did she suspect that he had known about the affair? It was true that she knew him well, and she had been friendly with his wife. Had Sally confided in her about her new relationship? Who knew? He could not ask her, for then he caste himself in the role of jealous husband, and this might make people look at him more closely. Could he confide in Katie? No, as much as he wanted to talk about what had happened with someone, he knew it was just too dangerous. He was finding living in the farmhouse with all his wife's and child's belongings heartbreaking. Sometimes he felt like he was going mad and living in a nightmare from which he couldn't wake up.

The only thing he could do was go about his normal business on the farm and hope that the police arrested someone for the murders very soon. He needed to look after Harry and make sure things were as normal as possible for him. He had started clearing out his wife and child's belongings and bagging up the toys and clothes that hurt him on a daily basis just by being there. His mother and father had said it was a bit soon to do this, but when was the right time? They suggested he wait awhile because he might regret getting rid of their things. And he noticed that Harry had taken a few of Joshua's little toys and squirrelled them away in his toy box. It was difficult to talk to him these days. He was so quiet and withdrawn. Not the noisy, boisterous seven-year-old he had once been.

After this was all over, they would go away for a while and decide together what kind of life they wanted going forward. Was Harry too young to help make such decisions? Bernard wasn't sure, but he knew he had to find a way to break through to his son.

The revelations about Sally that he had revealed, while going through her personal things were still weighing on his mind. There was so much he hadn't known about Sally and was that because he had failed to ask the right questions. He was not going to make the same mistake with his young son.

Chapter 46
The Inspector's Dilemma

This case was proving to be much trickier than even Inspector Lawrence had imagined. Now they had two men in police cells. Pete Douglas and Ahmed Burhan and the inspector had the feeling that neither of them was telling the truth. Perhaps the forensics would throw more light on who the culprit was. DNA samples had been taken from both men, and they were still waiting for the results. Even though Ahmed had confessed to the murders, he had said he did not sexually assault Sally.

It was possible that Sally's lover was not the killer and that what Ahmed was telling them was true, but the inspector had his doubts. On the one hand, the man had been in the area during all three of the murders, and the woman killed in the canal in London was very close to his flat. And in fact, they lived in the same building. He had confessed, and that counted for a lot, but some of his answers and the details he gave were sketchy. This could have been the language barrier, but Inspector Laurence was not convinced. The inspector had dealt with many murderers in the past, and the gruesome killing of Sally and her young son had been one of the most ferocious. Ahmed Burhan had come from a violent background and seen many atrocities, if his statement was to be believed, but he did not know the people he killed, and Sally and Joshua's murders struck the inspector as passionate and angry-personal even.

That was why the inspector was glad that Dr McDonald would be examining the prisoner the next morning. His colleagues were ready to throw their hands up and say they had caught the culprit, but in the inspector's eyes there were too many loose ends, and by abandoning the investigation at this point and concentrating on a conviction of Ahmed Burhan, this might mean that important evidence was missed. He trusted the doctor's instincts and felt that getting her input on the motivation and character of Mr Burhan would make things clearer for him.

Chapter 47
The Doctor

The doctor crossed her slim legs and opened her notebook. She did not rise as I entered the room but beckoned for me to enter and to take the seat opposite. I could feel her scrutiny as I took my seat opposite her. We were here to find out if I was mad or a monster. She did not smile but looked at me expectantly over the top of her glasses as if she were waiting for me to instigate the first exchange. It was an invitation but also a waiting game. People often feel uncomfortable with silence and so rush to fill it. I didn't feel the need to say anything, so I sat passively, patiently waiting for her to speak.

"Mr Burhan, do you know why you are here?" she asked eventually.

"Yes," I answered.

"And why is that?"

"To see if you think I am mad."

"Not exactly, but close enough," she replied.

"And do you think you are of sane mind?"

"No, not really."

"Why not?"

"Because people of sane mind do not go around killing people."

"You admit that you committed your crimes."

"Yes."

"Why did you do it?"

"I don't know, I thought you might have some ideas about that." He raised his eyebrows.

"Only you know what caused or motivated you to take the lives you have."

Ahmed looked at her from under his long, dark lashes and smiled.

"You know Mr Burhan, I am here to examine you on behalf of the Crown and to help them build their case against you. Once I have examined you, my report will be read to the court, and if you are found guilty, it may be used to decide on your sentencing."

Ahmed gave her a sly look. "So are you telling me I had better be careful about what I tell you?"

The doctor sat quietly for a moment as though contemplating and then decided to ignore his question.

"How do you feel about the deaths now?"

"Sorry and sad. I have seen the people in the newspapers and read about their lives, and I wish it had never happened. But it is no good wishing. What is done is done." Ahmed shrugged his shoulders.

"You don't feel any excitement, or perhaps you have flashbacks."

"I sometimes see the bodies of the mother and child in the cornfield and all that blood that was spilt, but I don't remember the actual killing."

"Let's leave the killing for the moment and go back to the beginning when you were a child. Tell me about your upbringing."

"I lived on a farm with my mother and father and my little sister Sacha."

"So have you always been an agricultural worker?"

"For most of my life, and then the war came, and our farm was confiscated, and my father went off to fight in the war. I was left to care for my mother and Sacha."

"Where are they now?"

"Dead. They were killed in the rebel wars when the army attacked Kabal."

"How old was your sister?"

"She was six."

"And your father."

"Dead also."

"How long is it since you lost your family?"

"My father died five years ago and mama and Sacha nearly two years."

"Would you say that their deaths affected you?"

"I wouldn't be here if it were not for their deaths. I didn't feel I could stay in Syria any longer. I wanted to get away, and that is why I became a refugee."

"How do you like living in England."

"It is not exactly going as well as I had hoped." He gave a slow, depreciative smile.

"Okay, Mr Burhan, we will leave it there for today, and I would like to see you again next week."

"Thank you. Will I be here next week?"

"I think that is likely, Mr Burhan. You are being held on remand until the case comes to trial."

The doctor got up and made her way to the door.

As an afterthought, I asked, "Dr McDonald are you

not ever scared when you are interviewing people as violent as me?"

"Do I have something to be scared about, Ahmed?"

"Well, prisoners might dislike your questions and not appreciate you prying into their lives."

"I will keep that in mind, Ahmed," she said as she closed her notebook.

The door closed with a click.

When he had left, Dr McDonald read through her notes to make sure they were legible and made sense so that her secretary could transcribe them later and put them in his file. There was something about Ahmed that made her uneasy. She had dealt with many hardened criminals in the past, but none like him. She couldn't quite put her finger on it. Some of them liked the drama of reliving their crimes; it gave them a buzz to talk about the gruesome details. There was shock value in telling the straight-laced doctor all the depraved things they had done. Sometimes Alison found it difficult not to let her disgust show on her face. To sit calmly while they described the most horrific crimes, but Ahmed did not seem to revel in his notoriety or want to boast about his cleverness. Instead, he seemed oblivious and on his guard, but also there was a sadness about him. A sign of an inner struggle; only time would tell. She was afraid that he might turn out to be one of the most complex cases she had come across.

Chapter 48
A Trick of the Light

Harry was alone in the house, and the farmhouse kitchen seemed huge and cold. The flagstone floor was dirty with crumbs and dust, and the rafters echoed with times past: Granny sitting by the fire in her high-backed armchair, telling him stories and making stew with dumplings at the large, open cooker. Mum making them laugh covered in flour from her baking and Joshua playing on the floor with his train set. Now he was left alone a lot while dad was out in the fields, or dealing with problems with the workers. He knew he could call dad at any time, and he was not far away. Hadn't dad bought him a new mobile phone and taught him how to use it carefully and patiently. But still Harry was afraid, scared of his own shadow, frightened when the windows rattled in the howling wind, worried when the old house creaked and groaned the way it had always done, but now it seemed more ominous. A knock at the door could send him scuttling to the toilet or coat cupboard where he could lock the door or hide amongst the coats. He tried to conceal his feelings as much as he could from grownups, but left to his own devices, he was anxious and on edge.

The therapist the school had called in to talk to him said it was natural to feel afraid after what had happened to his Mum and brother, but she didn't understand the sheer terror that came to him in his dreams and even in the waking hours of the night when he shook and sweat covered his body. He felt he was living in constant danger, but how could he tell dad that he didn't want to be left alone in the house when he had enough on his plate. Even as young as he was, he knew the farm would not run itself and although, most of the time, dad took him out to the fields when he was working, or tried to find someone to look after him after school. It was inevitable that at times he would have to be alone. The only place he felt safe was at grannies and grandpas, in their new bungalow, in town. Away from the farm and the memories of what had happened on the path just across the fields from where they lived. He longed to stay there with them and live in the little bedroom they had made for him, but dad refused to hear of it. Except when he had gone to London to help the police. He said he wanted Harry at home so he knew he was safe, and what could granny and grandpa say. They understood his feelings and could only go along with his wishes. Even when Harry cried and begged to be left with them they said, "No, you must do as your father says."

So this autumnal evening, as he sat at the large kitchen table, ostensibly doing his homework, but full of anxiety and foreboding, the knock on the door was terrifying. The loud noise seemed to drown everything out, and the sound of a man's voice that he didn't know filled him with fear.

"Is anyone home?" the voice called out, lifting the heavy doorknocker for the second time.

"It's Inspector Lawrence from the police."

Harry edged close to the window to see if the man was in a police uniform. He wasn't.

The inspector must have seen him. "Hello, Harry, isn't it? Is your dad home?"

It was too late to fall back out of sight. "No," Harry replied, trembling.

"He is out in the back field moving some wood."

"Okay, don't worry, I will call him on his mobile," the inspector replied.

He took out his phone and began to dial, but there was no reply, and he turned back to the front door.

"Could you possibly show me where he might be Harry?" the inspector cajoled. "He was very aware that he might be frightening the young boy. What if I put my identification badge through the letter box so that you can see I am a real policeman, or I could show you it through the window? Would that help?"

Harry nodded and said aloud, "Yes, I suppose so."

"All right then, here it is." The inspector held his badge up to the window.

Harry moved closer to get a better look and gingerly pulled the bolt back on the door.

"Thanks Harry. It is very sensible of you to be wary. Are you on your own then?"

"Dad is not far away." Harry did not want his dad to get in trouble by telling the policeman he was often left home alone.

"A tree came down in the high winds last week, and dad has chopped it up and is now taking it to the barn to store." His words came out in a rush.

"I see," said the inspector.

"And I had homework to do." He gestured to the maths books strewn across the kitchen table.

"Well, if you could take me to where your dad is working that would be great."

"We might be better heading for the barn, he is probably there by now."

"Fine," the inspector agreed.

Harry took his wellies from the stand outside the front door, and pulled on his big coat from the cupboard.

"Should we take the car or is the barn nearby?" the inspector asked.

"No, it is not far; we can walk," Harry replied.

As they navigated their way through the farmyard, the inspector had to slow his pace so the boy could keep up with him. He followed in Harry's footsteps down by the side of an old farm building, and halfway across another yard, the barn reared into view.

"There it is" – Harry said, pointing – "but I can't see dad's truck. Perhaps he is still up at the field."

They approached the barn, and Harry swung open the big door.

"Dad," he called as the inspector followed him inside.

There were various large machines obviously stored for when they were needed: attachments for tractors and trailers, an area where hay was stored and in the far corner, at the back of the barn, a store for the chopped wood where it was left to dry before being transported into the house for the open fire or used for wood chip.

Harry moved towards the wood store, with the

inspector close behind him, and just then the sun setting sent a shaft of light through the open door and shone straight onto an axe hanging on a beam with a host of other tools near the wood pile. The inspector's eyes were drawn immediately to the axe, and deep in his memory, something he had read about the murder weapon permutated into his consciousness. The blade had been worn at the far end, leaving a ridge in the cuts it had inflicted on its victims. And in a eureka moment, it occurred to him that perhaps he had been searching high and low for a murderer when the real culprit might have been a lot closer to home. He looked down at the boy by his side. He did not want to give anything away but did what he suspected mean the child was in danger.

"Come on, Harry, your dad's not here."

"Do you want me to take you out to the field we will have to go in your car it is quite a way."

"No Harry, that is okay," the inspector said as they went outside.

"It's getting dark, and you should be getting on with your homework. We will go back to the house, and if your dad is not back, you can ask him to give me a ring when he gets in."

Harry nodded, and they walked back through the farmyard, and even though the sun had set and there was a chill in the air, Harry felt safe with the inspector walking in step beside him. When they reached the door, Harry said, "Dad's truck isn't here. Do you want to come and wait inside?"

The inspector said no, he was going home for his tea

and not to forget to tell his dad to ring him, and he gave the boy his card.

"You know, Harry, if you are worried about anything you can call me on that number night or day," he said.

The boy's face brightened. "Really," he said.

"But aren't you really busy catching criminals?"

"Yes, but looking after people is part of my job too. So, if you are afraid or want to talk to someone, please do call."

Harry nodded. "Now go inside and lock the door until dad comes home."

The inspector turned to his car, and as he pulled away, he waved at Harry, who was looking from the window, having locked himself in quickly. Strange the inspector thought, he had come to the farm to tell Bernard Armstrong that they had a suspect for his wife and son's murder in custody. Only to be convinced that perhaps they were making a mistake, and the culprit was a lot closer to home. Of course the axe might not be the murder weapon, and even if it was, Bernard Armstrong might not be the man who killed Sally and Joshua. He had a number of men working on the farm alongside him, but the inspector was convinced that the investigation was taking a turn that he had not anticipated.

Half hour later, Harry's dad returned.

"Did you put all the wood in the barn?" Harry asked.

"No, I have left it covered in the back of the truck; it took me longer than I thought to load it. So, I will put it in the barn in the morning. Now what do you fancy for your tea? You must be starving." He looked over to the books

171

on the dining table. "Can you clear that lot away?"

"Yes, but I am not finished," Harry replied.

"Perhaps I can give you a hand after tea although you know Maths is not my strong point. Your..." He stopped midsentence.

"Mum was always better at numbers than you," Harry continued his father's train of thought.

"Yes, she was." Harry saw the tears in his father's eyes, and he felt bad for bringing Mum up. But they never talked about her or Joshua, and it made him sad like they had never existed. Even at such a young age, Harry thought it was just too difficult for them both to bear what they had lost. Because they had lost everything. And now there was just the two of them stuck in limbo, unable to help each other. He crossed the room to his father and hugged him around the waist. His father hugged him back and wiped away his tears.

"What about bangers and mash and beans?"

"That sounds good," Harry said through his sniffles.

Chapter 49
The Inspector

The trick of the light in the barn had made the inspector's brain wake up to the possibility that Bernard could be a suspect and that they had not looked into his movements, motives or alibi in any great depth because from the very start they had pigeonholed him as the grieving husband. One of the first rules of any enquiry was to look close to home and those closest to the victim. So why had they not done that in this instance? It was because of the other murder so close in time and kill site but had that just muddied the water.

What the inspector needed to do was to get a search warrant for the barn and the old farmhouse. There might be evidence there just waiting to be found, but did he have just cause? The judge would want to know that the warrant was not being obtained just for a fishing trip, as it was known. The family had suffered enough, and unless he could prove there was a reason to upset them further, he might not be successful. He decided he had to try. If it wasn't Bernard, it might be one of the farmhands or someone close to the family. They had taken statements from the men who worked alongside Bernard, but they had not been examined in any great detail as the hunt had been widened once the second victim was found.

This case was getting more and more complicated. There was Pete Douglas, who was keeping secrets and trying to protect his own hide, and there was the man Mr Douglas had heard in the back room with Sally. Both were suspects and now Ahmed Burhan was waiting to be questioned. He seemed to know a lot about the murders, but the inspector wasn't sure that most of what he knew couldn't be gleaned from the newspapers.

Thinking carefully about it, the inspector saw that Bernard had been the one to put Ahmed Burhan in the frame, and they had gone along with it. Was this his way of deflecting attention from himself. If so, he was playing a very clever game, and was Harry safe in his custody? The inspector wasn't a man who believed in signs, but it seemed to him that someone or somebody was trying to help him unravel this case. Call it divine intervention or a trick of the light, but that axe in the barn had been lit up just as they opened the door. All along they had thought the murderer would have disposed of the murder weapon, but what if he just hid it in plain sight?

The inspector's tea would have to wait, he thought, as he headed back to the station to apply for the search warrant. What did he have to lose? Something wasn't right, and if he didn't do something about it, he wouldn't be sleeping tonight.

Once he reached the station, he was pleased to see that the forensic report was sitting on his desk. The DNA from the victim's body showed that there was sexual activity the morning of the murder, and the samples from the men in custody were not a match. Neither Pete nor Ahmed Burhan had been Sally's lover. Now he needed to get a sample from her husband and the man Pete Douglas had heard in the back room of the farm shop. They might not be the murderer, but a clearer picture of what was happening in Sally's life might emerge.

He also rang the tech department to see where they were with Sally's telephone. It had been badly smashed in the attack, but the department had been working on restoring the memory.

"We have managed to retrieve some text messages from the phone," the technician informed the inspector. "I will send over what we have found, but there are a number of messages from someone who signs himself J. And let's just say it doesn't seem to be a platonic relationship."

"Thanks, Dave, have you been able to identify the telephone number of the sender?"

"Yes, it is a London number."

"Right, well, that would tally with other information we have. Send me over what you have straight away."

Inspector Lawrence wasn't sure what to do with this new information. Did Bernard Armstrong know that his wife was being unfaithful and had it made him so jealous he had killed her, or was he unaware of his wife's secret life? There was only one way to find out; he would have to ask him, but not before he had checked the texts and the telephone number of the sender and paid him a visit. A follow up meeting with Bernard Armstong would have to sit on the back burner for a while. Once the warrant had been issued, they would take him in for questioning. In the meantime, the inspector waited for the text messages to be sent over, and then, having gleaned the telephone number of the sender and got a colleague to find out his details, he put in a call to Jack.

"Good afternoon, Mr Harris. This is Inspector Lawrence, of the Metropolitan Police, and I am leading the enquiry into the murder of Sally and Joshua Armstrong."

Jack had been expecting this call or a knock on the door for the past few months, and now it had come, he had no idea how to play this.

"Good afternoon," Jack managed to respond. He was determined to give away nothing.

"I understand that you knew Sally Armstrong."

Jack thought about his answer carefully, should he admit to the relationship or wait to see what the police had?

"Are you there, Mr Harris."

"Yes, inspector. What makes you think I knew a Sally Armstrong, and what is this all about?"

The inspector was losing patience with the man. "I am sure you know that Sally and her son were murdered. We have Mrs Armstrong's phone, Mr Harris, and there are a number of texts between you two that we have been able to access."

"Right," this was Jack's worse nightmare; he had thought for a long while that Sally's phone could really incriminate him, and now the police had it.

"I think it would be best, Mr Harris, if you came into the police station at nine a.m. tomorrow morning to help us with our enquiries."

"Do I need a lawyer."

"That is up to you, sir. You are not being charged with

anything yet."

The inspector gave Jack the address of the police station and told him he expected to see him the following day.

As the inspector hung up, he wondered if he should have sent police officers round to Jack Harris's house. How did he know he wouldn't try to abscond? All they had were text messages at the moment, but these could be key, and once they had Mr Harris in custody, they could request a DNA sample for which they would need his co-operation. He would see what the morning would bring.

Chapter 50
The Game is Up

As Jack replaced the receiver, a thousand thoughts went through his head. How was he to keep all this from his wife? Although he knew he had nothing to do with the murder, just being involved in the enquiry would be enough to upset Lydia. And maybe give her a reason to end their marriage. He knew nothing about what happened to Sally and her son, and he had to make the inspector see that. Who knew he might be persuaded to keep his involvement quiet? For now, he would have to think about exactly what he was going to tell the police and that could be tricky. Should he be completely honest or make it sound like the relationship was over? What he needed to do was find out exactly what they knew. He thought about the texts he had sent Sally and scrolled through his phone to see if he could shed a better light on the messages he had sent her. As he looked through them, he realised that many were quite explicit; there was no way of sugarcoating their relationship. It was obvious they were lovers, and perhaps if he was straight with the police and threw himself on their mercy, they might not feel the need to publicise the fact that he had been questioned, and Lydia might never know. He tried to feel optimistic about the situation, but he had a sinking feeling that he was finally going to get caught out and held accountable for all his past indiscretions.

In the meantime, the inspector had obtained the search warrant he had been waiting for and was heading with a team of forensic experts to the farm. They were lucky to find Bernard at home making Harry's breakfast. Two steaming bowls of porridge were sitting on the table, but the inspector made no apologies for interrupting. He waved the warrant in Bernard's face and noted the shocked look.

"What is all this about?" he asked.

"We need to search the house, the barn and the outbuildings, Mr Armstrong. And you need to provide me with a list of all the people who were working on the farm on the day of the murder."

"Okay, inspector, but can we do this when Harry has gone to school?"

"I am afraid not, Mr Armstrong; I suggest you call your parents to pick Harry up and take him to school. You are needed here."

Bernard's parents arrived within twenty minutes and were quick to shepherd the boy out of the door and off to school with a "call me" from Bernard's mum as she left him looking a grey colour.

The police officers went from room to room looking in drawers and thoroughly searching every cupboard and area of the house. Three men were dispatched to the barn to examine the tools and the axe that had made such an impression on the inspector the last time he had visited. Everything was bagged up meticulously, and every care was taken not to contaminate the evidence. It could come down to these objects to get a conviction for the murder.

"I would like you to accompany me down to the station," the inspector told Bernard once Harry was safely dispatched with the grandparents.

"I would rather stay here and see what this lot are up to," Bernard complained.

"I am sure you would, but that was not a request. We will let them get on with their job, and we will go to the station for an interview."

"Am I being arrested?" Bernard asked crossly.

"No, not unless you refuse to come along with me," the inspectors tone conveyed that he would take no arguments.

Bernard went and grabbed his coat and followed the inspector to a waiting car. He took one last look at the farmhouse and wondered when he would see it again. He had no idea what sort of evidence the police had, but the inspector's attitude towards him had completely changed, and that could not be good. He was no longer being treated with the respect for a grieving husband but with the determination and tone of a policeman on a case that he wanted to solve.

At the police station Bernard was taken to an interview room and left there for a while, not knowing what was going on. At least they hadn't taken him straight to a cell, he thought. All he had to do was hold his nerve. He rehearsed in his head the details of his alibi for the day of Sally and Joshua's murders. When the inspector finally began to ask his questions, he was clear and precise about where he had been, who he had seen and called. He was pleased with himself and the way he had answered the questions, but then the inspector asked him about Sally's relationship with her lover, and he had to try and look shocked and unaware that the affair had been going on even if underneath his blood was boiling.

"Let's cut to the chase, Mr Armstrong, you knew your wife was cheating, and you decided to kill her."

"That's ridiculous, Inspector, I loved my wife, and I don't believe she was having an affair."

"I put it to you that you found out she was cheating, and you confronted her about it and killed her cold bloodedly with the axe you keep in the barn."

All Bernard's fears were coming true. The inspector had pieced together what had happened completely.

"What I don't understand is why you killed that innocent child."

Bernard found the tears springing to his eyes and could not control them. He wiped them with the back of his hand.

"I refuse to say another word until I have spoken to my lawyer."

The inspector had expected Bernard to ask for his lawyer early on and was not surprised by this turn of events.

"That is your right. You will be kept in the cells until he arrives."

Bernard was led out by a large police officer and taken downstairs to the cells for a long wait.

How had everything turned into this terrible situation so quickly, he wondered as he put his head in his hands and sobbed.

Chapter 51

Jack's interview was going just as badly. A DNA test was taken as soon as he arrived, and from the beginning he felt like he was very much a suspect in the case. The police officers who dealt with him seemed hostile and disbelieving of everything he told them. He tried to spin it that he and Sally were a casual thing and that he knew nothing about the horrific murder until he saw it on the Internet. But they looked at him as if they had heard it all before, and he was made to go over the events leading up to the murder in minute detail over and over again. The visit to the hotel, where they had met, his movements when he left the area, and where he had gone. He had told them he had stopped for petrol on the way home and called on a client in Peterborough. Hopefully they would check these facts and he would be off the hook. He knew that his DNA would have put him with Sally that morning, the morning of her death, but that did not mean he had killed her. He had to make them see that he was innocent. But even to himself, his answers sounded flimsy. He was the last one to see her alive apart from the murderer, and they would be able to prove they had a relationship when the forensics came back. That was when he knew he had to call a solicitor and that his wife was going to find out about his affair. Jack's world was about to fall apart, and there was nothing he could do about it. The reality was that he had to stay out of prison, that was the main objective, and in the storm that was about to be unleashed, he might end up losing his wife and the life he had known.

"So is there anything you want to add to your statement, Mr Harris?" the detective asked.

"No, I don't think so," Jack replied. He had been in the Police Station for over five hours and had no expectation of being released soon.

"Okay, then you are free to go, but please do not leave the area without telling the police where you are going. No holidays planned, have we?"

"No. No."

"Right, so we know where you are should we need you to help with our enquiries further."

"Yes." Jack gathered his belongings and got out of there as quickly as he could before they changed their minds. He didn't know what was going on, and he hadn't expected to be let go, but he had the feeling that was not the last he had seen of Detective Lawrence.

Outside in the fresh air, he had the urge to run for the hills, but he knew that would just make him seem guilty. What should he tell Lydia? Would it be better to tell her he had been in to speak to the police about a murder, but how much should he divulge? Would it be more prudent to tell Lydia about his relationship with Sally before the police did, or should he keep it to himself in the hope that they would not follow up this line of enquiry. He knew he was being a bit optimistic, if not naive. This was not just going to go away.

Chapter 52
The Aftermath

After sitting in the hotel car park for about an hour, I decided to go home. There was no point in sitting there if I wasn't going in to confront them, and I did not want to be caught when Sally came out and started to make her way home. What I needed was time to think. Was I going to tell her I knew about her seedy little affair, or was I going to continue as if nothing had happened? Was that even possible in the state I was in? I didn't think so. But I did not want to lose my wife or my family. I thought about talking to someone about it but the only person I could think of was Katie, and she was Sally's friend as well as mine. And what could I say anyway? "My wife is being unfaithful."

It seemed such a cliché, and what could she say, "Oh, I am so sorry." That wouldn't help. No, what was needed was action, and at the moment I had the element of surprise, as Sally did not know I knew. It was just what form that action should take.

At home in the farmhouse, I poured myself a stiff whisky and found myself pacing up and down the flagstoned kitchen. Periodically I would look out of the kitchen window to see if Sally was coming along the lane towards the house, but there was no sign of her. Then I remembered she had to pick Joshua up from school. Even so, she was a little late; perhaps she had gone for coffee with one of the other mothers or they had stopped at the local park so the children could let off steam on the way home. I felt like a caged animal in an enclosed space, so I slipped on my donkey jacket and headed out towards the barn across the open fields. I needed to clear my head. I knew I wasn't the kind of man who could just live with this secret; it would eat away at me, and I would be suspicious of her every move. I didn't want to lose her, but I didn't know if our marriage could survive her infidelity. It was no good I was going to have to confront her. Come what may, I needed to bring her dirty secret out in the open to know if she intended to continue seeing this man or if she wanted to stay with me and our family. I felt the tears begin to fall, and I brushed them aside with the sleeve of my coat. I couldn't believe our wonderful marriage had come to this. My anger was giving way to a pain in my chest that wouldn't seem to shift. I couldn't contemplate a life without Sally and the children.

Out at the barn, I picked up the axe and made my way over to a large trunk of an oak tree that had come down in the recent storms. I would start chopping it up for firewood that would help me occupy the time until Sally returned and give me time to think. But what was there to think about? I chopped the wood; it was hard work, and then I moved all the logs over to the side of the field for transporting later to the barn or woodshed to store them and give them a chance to dry out. The branches and debris needed to be removed if we were going to use the field for the sheep. The task kept me occupied physically, but as I worked up a sweat, I wondered what I was doing this for. Would my family still be here in the winter? Nothing seemed worthwhile.

I stuck the axe inside my coat and decided to go and meet Sally and Joshua. I walked across the fields towards the neighbouring farm, they may have taken a short cut across the fields rather than coming down the usual lanes. They used the public footpaths, which wound around the perimeters of our land and the farm next door. In the summer months, this was a nicer way to walk home, and they often stopped to pick wild flowers in the meadow. It wasn't long before I could see the outline of the two blonde figures in the distance. Dark clouds were starting to gather overhead, and I could feel the anger within me growing the closer I got towards them. Perhaps I should turn around and go home before I did something I would regret, I thought to myself. But still I walked on thinking about what she had been up to that very afternoon, and then she just carried on as normal and went to the school and picked up our son. Should I ask her where she had been and who with? Was that the way to go, but what was the point? I knew the answer. Part of me wanted to know all the gory details of the liaison, and part of me wanted to just shut it out. And then there we were face to face, and reason flew out of the window. She opened her mouth to talk, and before I knew it, I took the axe out of my coat, and in a frenzy of anger, I killed them both there, where they stood. There was no time for explanations, lies or deceit. I did not give her the chance to defend herself, and she did not see it coming. It was just good old Bernard coming to meet them both on the way home. They smiled at me as I approached; Joshua was pleased to see me, and Sally had a quizzical look on her face as if to say, 'This is unexpected,' and it was.

Later, I wondered if I had intended to kill them when I put the axe inside my coat and made my way across the fields. I have decided that in a sub-conscious way I must have; otherwise, why did I take the axe instead of returning it to the barn where it belonged? Why did I kill my innocent little son, and my only answer is because he was there and I knew that he could identify me? What a monster I hear you saying, and I am that and more. I know that. Divorce would have been far simpler. I realise that now, but I wasn't thinking straight. I was jealous and angry, and I couldn't see past the red mist in my head to punish her. That was what it came down to, but once that mist had passed and I saw the damage I had done, the only thing to do then was to survive, to make sure no one found out, and the best way to do that was to find another suspect – someone else to blame.

It was only when I went to London and saw Ahmed that the idea occurred to me that the refugee would be an ideal candidate. And I have to say that the second murder on my part was a stroke of genius. Everyone knows that in murder cases the police always look close to home, but the killing of the old lady on her bike made them think they had a killer on the loose, someone who was targeting women in the area, and so it shifted the investigation away from the grieving husband. Yes, definitely a stroke of genius.

Chapter 53
Bernard

As the blood ran down the sink, Bernard turned his hands over and over, scrubbing them red raw to get rid of the gore of his actions. Then he took off his clothes where he stood and put them in the washing machine in the utility room. He made the way up to the bathroom and let the shower run hot before getting in and cleaning every inch of his body. In just over an hour, Harry would be coming out of school, and he had to hold himself together and wait until the school rang to say that Sally had not arrived to pick him up. The axe had been safely hidden back in the big barn. He had washed it, wiped it clean, and hung it back up in its usual place. Should he dispose of it later? Just in case the police searched the place. Its blade might be quite distinctive, having been used for various tasks around the farm. Yes, he decided for the moment it might be okay, but he did need to get rid of it. An alibi that was his next step; where was he today? He picked up his phone and rang the feed merchant and ordered some sugar beet for the sheep. Then he rang Katie and was going to ask her if she had seen Sally, as he would have if she was usually late home. There was no answer. Those were two calls the police could trace. Next he got on his bright red tractor and rode on it to the field nearest the road, where a number of people would probably recall seeing him. He called out a greeting to his nearest neighbour, Brian Smart, and then headed back to the farmhouse to wait for the call from the school. In fact, it was the police who called first, having found the bodies of Sally and Joshua. Later he learnt that his mother had been asked to collect Harry by the school when they could not get hold of Bernard.

The police had treated him like a grieving husband and father from the start, and he had no problems playing that role. After all, he had loved both Sally and Joshua. If his answers to the police's questioned seemed sketchy, they put it down to the shock of such a terrible, violent crime being committed against the people he loved. His tears were genuine, for when he saw them again, he realised the enormity of what he had done, but although he felt regret, the one overwhelming emotion was the need to get away with his crime. Whatever happened, he needed to cover his tracks. Killing the elderly lady on her bicycle had been a master stroke of genius, he felt. Early evening he had followed her until she had stopped for a rest. Parking up a good way from her and keeping out of sight, he had managed to take her unaware and kill her almost silently. It was surprisingly easy. If he was to get away with his first crime, he had to throw the spotlight somewhere else, and if the police felt there was a serial killer on the loose, they were less likely to look at the victim's husband.

When he thought back to when he realised Sally was being unfaithful, his first plan had been to kill both her and her lover. But as he began to turn this over in his head, he realised that it might be better to leave the lover alive and have him be the one who was blamed for the killing. The funny thing was no one had come forward to say that Sally was having an affair and meeting her lover at the Swan Hotel outside town. He had been sure that a member of staff at the hotel would recognise Sally perhaps on the news and come forward to say where she had been just before the murder. And the police had not really shown much interest in piecing together her whereabouts directly before the murder. They knew she had been to the school in the morning and had visited Katie before setting off for home with Joshua, but no one had mentioned the hour's in-between and the lover had never been questioned. Bernard began to see that Sally being seen as a dutiful wife and not an adulterous harlot might work in his favour. His family's reputation would not be tarnished, and if they seemed to be blissfully happy, there was no reason for the police to suspect him of the murder. The terrible thing was Bernard had never meant to kill Joshua. His original plan was to confront Sally before she left for the school and picked up Joshua. But having got back to the farm and retrieved his axe from the barn he realised that Sally was not coming home but going directly to the school for the lunchtime pickup. He had to abandon his idea of a home invasion or burglary gone wrong and think on his feet. In fact, he wasn't thinking clearly at all; he was so enraged and angry at the idea of her unfaithfulness and the realisation that he could lose his children and his home that he had recklessly set out to confront her. But something went wrong when he saw her; all reason flew out of the window; all he could think was that she was a conniving, lying bitch, and before he knew it, he had wiped that less than innocent smile off her face. No words were exchanged; she had looked up pleased to see him, but in the horror of the moment, he had looked down at Joshua and realised he had witnessed what he had done and there was no going back. He had killed him with one sweep of the axe. It was something he had to live with the look in his innocent eyes as he looked up at his father.

It wasn't until his visit to London when he saw Ahmed down by the canal that he considered framing someone else for the murders. After all he recognised the refugee from his walk backwards and forwards to the supermarket taking the route along the road at the side of the fields where he worked. He knew that he was from the area, and the likelihood was that he had been in the area around the time Sally and Joshua were killed. All he needed to do was bring him to the attention of the police and then implicate him in a murder in London. What could have been easier than to kill someone who lived in his flats – the jogger as she ran along the canal near Ahmed's home? It had all just fallen into place, as if it was meant to be. No one would believe that a local, well-respected farmer would kill his own beautiful wife and child, but a refugee – that was another matter. That was something local people would find it easy to believe. Bernard had heard people talking about the newcomers in the local pub, and most were wary of them.

Chapter 54
Later

It seems like a dream. The psychiatrist says I didn't kill all those people – Sally and her child, the woman down by the canal in London, the old lady on her bike in Sussex. She says I am suffering from Post-Traumatic Stress after the death of my mother and sister. I have a form of mental illness, and seeing these terrible events in the news and papers, I have become confused and believed that I have killed these people. I have convinced myself that I am responsible when really it was someone else. Someone who the police have now caught. How can this be? Why was I running away if I didn't hurt anyone? It would be wonderful to be absolved from all these terrible events if I could only believe that this is the case.

They have me taking very strong drugs here. Sometimes I do not know if I am hallucinating or not. But the psychiatrist says that in time I will come off the drugs and that she has every confidence that I will make a full recovery. Just imagine I might have the chance to start again in my new country without the fear of being caught or running from town to town. That is, if the psychiatrist is real and not just a figment of my imagination.